Philly Girl 2:

Carl Weber Presents

Philly Girl 2:

Carl Weber Presents

Marcus Weber

www.urbanbooks.net

Urban Books, LLC
300 Farmingdale Road, N.Y.-Route 109
Farmingdale, NY 11735

Philly Girl 2: Carl Weber Presents

ISBN 13: 978-1-64556-280-1
ISBN 10: 1-64556-280-8

First Trade Paperback Printing February 2022
Printed in the United States of America

10 9 8 7 6 5 4 3 2 1

Distributed by Kensington Publishing Corp.
Submit Orders to:
Customer Service
400 Hahn Road
Westminster, MD 21157-4627
Phone: 1-800-733-3000
Fax: 1-800-659-2436

Philly Girl 2:

Carl Weber Presents

by

Marcus Weber

Chapter 1

Isis was lying on the ground, trying her best to slow down the bleeding coming from the buck-fifty cut running down her face. She screamed in pain. The open wound on her face was burning. It felt like a red-hot poker being pressed against her face. The bystanders stood around, filming and taunting. Nobody wanted to get close enough to help.

Rita walked away with the razor blade still in her hand, unfazed by Isis's loud cries.

What started as a fist fight ended up with Rita upping the stakes, giving Isis a permanent reminder of why you should never disrespect or bite the hand that feeds you. Rita was the boss. You never cross the boss. Isis needed to remember such things. Especially at this point in time. Rita was expanding her empire from West Philly into North Philly. There was no forgiveness in Rita's world while she was executing her plans for a complete takeover of Philly.

Rita inherited money, drugs, and guns from her pops, Big Wink. When the Feds grabbed a hold of him and gave him a life sentence for drug trafficking and other violent crimes, Rita took over his spot. She was only seventeen when he got locked up. By the time she turned twenty, she had her hands heavy in the drug game.

It took a long time for people to take her seriously. There weren't too many niggas in the hood that were about to let a chick run the streets. They didn't care that her father was Big Wink. She had to earn her respect amongst the men, and that's exactly what she did. It really didn't take much but a few shootouts here, a few shootouts there, a couple of bar fights, and a boyfriend she left paralyzed from the waist down after he put his hands on her.

On the flip side, she looked out for a lot of people and fed a lot of families in the hood. She threw parties almost every weekend and made sure the bar was open every time she stepped foot in the place. Oftentimes, she would pull a school bus up to the corner and give out toys, clothes, and other gifts to the children in the neighborhood. Rita took so much away from the hood that the only thing she could do in return was give back. She wanted to give back as much as she could.

It was bitches like Isis who ruined a good time. She displayed her disrespect and disloyalty to Rita in an outward manner, leaving people to believe that Rita had softened up. Isis worked for Rita, selling crack. On a few occasions, Isis would take the flip money and score more coke from a different supplier, then sell the bullshit coke on Rita's corner during the night shift. She stayed under the radar for a couple of months, until the crackheads started complaining about the product. Rita got wind of that information fast and immediately pulled up on Isis during the nighttime activities.

"Yo, what's up, Isis?" Rita stepped out of her car.

"Oh, yo. What brings you out here tonight? Ain't you got no party or something to go to?" Isis smiled.

"Nah. Just coming to check on my girl."

"A'ight. That's what's up. You know I love seein' my cousin."

Rita stood next to Isis on the corner. "How's business?"

"Good, good." Isis nodded.

"Let me see what you working with tonight."

"You sure? I don't think it's best to do this out in the open."

Rita's voice was stern. "What you mean? You handing fiends their package on this corner. Am I right? I'm not to the level of a fiend?" she said. "Let me see my shit."

Isis reluctantly reached into her pocket and pulled out a vial and handed it to Rita.

"What's this? This don't look like my packaging."

"Ah, yeah, yeah. You see, I ran out of your tops, so I had to improvise. Used my own."

Rita ripped the razor blade down the side of Isis's face, opening a huge, Grand Canyon-shaped, bloody gash.

In Rita's mind, Isis got off easy because she was Rita's older cousin. If it were anybody else, Rita would have just sent someone to kill her. But for Rita, family was everything.

"Somebody take dis bitch to the hospital," Rita said openly to whoever was out there. She walked toward the corner of 60th and Market Street, the razor dripping blood.

It didn't take long for somebody to act on her demand. When she wanted something done, it got done, and everybody who rolled with her immediate camp was willing to roll out for her in any cause.

Rita sat on the edge of her 2007 BMW 650i underneath the train tracks. She looked up at the El train going by. The sparks it spit from the tracks rained down like a Fourth of July fireworks display. She wasn't feeling guilty about cutting her cousin's face, but she was upset that her weekend party started in an hour, and the blood from Isis's face had gotten all over her clothes. She hated being late, especially to her own parties.

She looked down at her bloody outfit. "Shit. I looked fly, too."

***

"Nigga, I'ma ask you one more time only. After that, I'ma start doin' shit to you that's gonna make you wish you complied the first time," Dave told Rich, who was lying on the bed.

Rich was still in shock and somewhat still asleep, looking down the barrel of a large revolver. His hands and feet had been tied together. Rich could have sworn he saw the bullet down the barrel of the gun before duct tape was put over his eyes. His girlfriend, Megan, had been stripped naked, and his three-year-old daughter lay asleep next to him in the bed.

He wondered how three armed gunmen had gotten into his condo in a gated community. The security was pretty good, and the armed guard at the front gate made things difficult—that is, until Dave caught Megan slipping, coming from the club. She was the only access Dave had to getting past the guard, or for that matter, getting into the condo without the alarm going off.

Dave, Lump, and Cees were probably the most intelligent stickup boys in the city of Philadelphia. They were accurate and very well put together, and if you became their target, then there was pretty much no escaping the confrontation. Their main, and pretty much only, targets were big-time drug dealers who thought they couldn't be touched. Those kinds of drug dealers proved to be the easiest ones to rob, especially if they had something to live for, let's say, like a family.

"Where da fuck is the money and drugs?" Dave asked in his calmest voice while leaning over the bed and tapping Rich on the forehead with the barrel of his gun.

Rich thought about it for a second. He knew he and his family weren't going to make it out of this situation alive, and the only thing he had as leverage was 200K and a few bricks of cocaine. He wasn't really worried about himself.

All he wanted was to get his family out of the house safely and in one piece.

"Yo, I got like 200K and a couple of bricks, but I'm not giving up nothing until you let my girl and my daughter go," he said. "You can do whatever you want to me. Just let them go. Other than that, you might as well kill us all and don't get shit!"

Dave went into the kitchen where Lump and Cees were sitting at the table. This was the normal routine. They always did the muscle part of the job, then Dave did all the talking and negotiating. Dave just had a way of making people come up off their money.

"What y'all niggas talking about?" he asked while sitting down at the table with his chair facing the bedroom so he could keep an eye on Rich.

"Yo, man, I been meaning to tell you that I got a crazy lick for us after this," Lump announced while leaning back in his chair. "I got to do a little more homework on it, but I know for a fact that we can clear like 500K and some work."

"From what I heard so far, it sounds like a good sting that could allow us to sit back for a couple months," Cees chimed in, giving Dave a nod of approval.

It was crazy that Dave, Lump, and Cees were sitting in the middle of a robbery with the possibility of murder, discussing their next hit. They acted as though this was their house, and it didn't bother them that they had three hostages duct-taped in the next room.

"Well, entertain me," Dave said. He walked over to the bar and grabbed a bottle of whiskey off the shelf. It was a rare vintage that cost thousands of dollars. Dave had no idea. He was a bottom feeder who knew nothing of the finer things in life. He unscrewed the top and placed the bottle in the center of the table.

"Look. It's this chick out in West Philly getting a lot of money, and the camp she's rollin' wit' is weak. My man said she's worth like a million easy, and that's not including the coke she may have lyin' around."

"A chick?" Dave asked, making sure that he heard Lump right.

"Yeah, dog, a chick."

Dave took a swig of the whiskey and passed it to Cees. He glanced over into the bedroom to make sure that Rich or his wife hadn't moved. Rich was struggling to break free of his restraints. Rick's wife and daughter were huddled together, crying.

The lick almost sounded too good to be true, but he had confidence in Lump to make sure that the homework was done on a job before they put it to the test. That's one thing that Lump was good at. He would sit on a job for days at a time, learning his victim's every move, to the point that he'd know what they were going to do before they did it.

"Yo, it's whatever, Lump. You do the homework and get back wit' me by the middle of next week. Cees, you roll wit' me this weekend so we can get rid of the coke we have left over from the last job," Dave directed. "After this sting, we're going to fall back for a couple of months and enjoy the rest of the summer."

Everyone was in agreement with the idea of taking off for a couple of months. They'd been working all spring, and with June a mere thirty-five days away, ballin' out of control for the summer sounded like a great idea. New cars, fast bikes, fast women, hotel parties, club hopping, and maybe even a vacation to the tropics were just some of the things that Dave and his boys looked forward to. By September, it would be right back to work, though. Back on the grind and making that paper. Well, not making that paper, but taking that paper. These three didn't know the meaning of work. They constantly played the victim and blamed their hardships on everyone else but themselves. Personal responsibility wasn't in their vocabulary.

"So, what about him?" Lump asked, nodding in the direction of the room that Rich and his wife were in.

"Oh, shit! I almost forgot," Dave said, coming back to the reality of the current situation. "He said he got 200K and a couple of bricks, but he wants us to let his wife and kid go first before he gives us anything."

"That nigga willing to die for his family. Respect," Lump said.

"They seen our faces. None of 'em should live," Cees said.

"I ain't down to kill no child," said Lump.

"Me neither," Dave said.

"So, what we gonna do? I ain't getting locked up." Cees raised his voice.

"Chill. Let me think. There's a way we can do this." Dave closed his eyes so there was no distraction while he went over different scenarios. "I got it." He opened his eyes.

Dave went back into the room to Rich to discuss the terms they came up with. When he returned to the room, the little girl, who was asleep in the bed next to Rich, had woken up and was sitting up in the bed. She looked Dave right in the eyes before climbing behind her father as though she was hiding.

Megan just cried out behind her duct-taped mouth, wishing they'd just take what they wanted and leave.

"Look, Rich, I got some good news and some bad news. The good news is I'ma let you live," Dave said, taking a seat on the bed next to him. "The bad news is that I got to kill ya wife, because she saw me and my guys' faces. I can't let her live. I'm sorry."

Megan screamed out again from behind the duct tape at the thought of being killed in front of her daughter. It was bad enough that she had to die, but doing it in front of the baby was just downright cruel.

"Now, the decision is up to you. I could kill everybody in the room and leave with nothing, or I could just kill her, and you and ya daughter can live. You might be broke, but you'll raise ya daughter."

Rich didn't even have to think about it. His mind was made up the minute the deal was offered. "The money is behind the stove, and the coke is in the bathroom cupboard," Rich said, then screamed out to Megan that he was sorry. He hated to see her die, but there was no need for everybody to go if he could help it. That's just the price you pay playing the game.

Rita sat in her reserved VIP booth at the Arch Street Club, sipping her usual drink of orange juice on the rocks. She needed to be clear in the head in order to be the boss bitch she knew she was; therefore, she didn't drink alcohol or smoke weed. Her drug of choice was money. She loved getting a lot of it and doing it at a fast rate.

The club was packed tonight, much like every Friday, but even with all the people there, Rita felt alone. Since her last abusive boyfriend and the way their relationship turned out, it was hard for her to find anyone on her level. It wasn't about the money with her. She wanted someone who had the same morals and goals she had. She wanted someone who was loyal, respectful, truthful, and honest; gentle when needed and rough when necessary. Someone who could fuck the shit out of her in the afternoon, then love her at night, fulfilling every sexual desire her mind and body could come up with. At times, she thought that she was asking for too much in a man, but every morning, she woke up and took a look in the mirror, realizing that she deserved a good man.

Aside from cutting chicks' faces, Rita was a very beautiful young woman. She stood five foot six, weighing 145 pounds, and had a light-brown complexion with shoulder-length hair. Her stomach was flat, she had 36B breasts, and her ass wasn't flat, but it wasn't fat. She was like a 9, and the only reason that she wasn't a dime was because of the way her eyes would cross every once in a while. Even then, she was wifey material, probably the baddest chick in the club.

"Girl, you gonna get up and dance?" her best friend, Shay asked, stumbling over to the booth. "You been sitting here all night. If you sit here any longer, you're gonna turn into a cushion for the booth!" she joked.

Rita was there, but her mind was in ten different places at one time. She was running low on coke, and it was time to re-up before the new month started. This problem was becoming all too frequent. She'd started using a new supplier, Basco, and he was consistently late with shipments and always had some excuse as to why. It was getting on Rita's nerves.

It was a headache dealing with Basco. He always had something going on with the prices, and at times she felt like he was trying to play her because she was a female. These were the times that she wished she had a man in her life who understood the street aspect of the game.

"You know, I got to go see Basco in a couple of days," she said, looking off into the club and getting into her business mode. "We're running low, and the first of the month is on Tuesday."

"Re-Re, don't stress. I'ma set everything up wit' Basco. Me and Matt can take care of the buy, and you can finally take a break for a change," Shay said, seeing her best friend drained from the streets.

Shay wasn't just Rita's best friend. She was her younger half-sister. They had the same father but different mothers and grew up together under the same roof with Big Wink. Shay was like the underboss. Any and everything Rita did, she knew about it. She was probably the only person Rita would trust with her life, and it wasn't because she was her sibling, but because she had earned that trust through the years.

"Look. Y'all just chill here. I'ma go home and get some rest. I'm not really feeling the club thing tonight," Rita said, checking her pocketbook for her car keys. "I'ma give you a call in the morning so we can go out and do something."

"Yo, you sure you don't need me to ride wit' you?" Shay asked, a little concerned about her attitude.

"Naw, I'm good, girl. You enjoy ya'self tonight. I'll see you tomorrow," she said and headed for the exit.

Chapter 2

Isis walked out of the hospital and jumped right in the car with Matt. He had driven her to the hospital the night before and stayed with her. After Rita cut Isis, Matt was the only one who volunteered to drive her to the hospital. He'd known Isis for a few years. They'd seen each other around the neighborhood and began talking. If Matt had his way, they'd be dating. He liked Isis but couldn't tell if she was into him. He wanted to fuck real bad.

When she got into the car, Matt could see that Isis was hot. The four-inch cut running down the left side of her face looked crazy, especially since Isis was one of the baddest chicks in the hood. The cut went so deep that it didn't require stitches but rather a countless amount of staples in order to keep the wound closed.

"Are you good?" Matt asked, looking over at Isis before putting the car in drive.

Hell no, Isis wasn't cool. She was on fire about the whole situation. This wasn't just some random act by a jealous chick Isis was used to arguing with. This happened at the hands of her own cousin—actual blood cousin, at that. Rita's dad and Isis's dad had the same mother but different fathers, which made the girls first cousins and stepsisters. She couldn't believe family would do her like that over some money.

"Yeah, I'm good," Isis replied, flipping down the sun visor to look in the mirror.

The whole left side of her face was red, and just looking at what would be a permanent scar triggered something inside of her. It was like a pit bull that got bit for the first time, then turned into a killing machine. At that point, that very moment, she looked at her face for the first time and snapped. This situation was far from over with. Isis wasn't going to lay down and take this on the chin like Rita expected. After all, they both came from the same blood line, and neither one of their fathers fell short of being a gangsta.

"Dis bitch can't be serious," Isis mumbled, flippin' the mirror back up. "She got me fucked up."

"Yo, I don't know what you expected, Isis. You already know how Rita is, especially when it comes to stealing from her."

"I didn't steal shit from her!" Isis shouted out in anger. "The little extra stuff I was selling on the side came from my money, not hers."

"Yeah, but you selling it on her corner. Not only that, but you didn't even buy the coke from her," Matt said, not taking his eyes off the road.

"Her corner? Her corner?" Isis asked. "I don't see dat bitch standing out there for sixteen hours a day or controlling the traffic that comes through there. Yeah, she supplies us, but I run that corner. Her money is never short when she comes to collect. What I do on my free time, wit' my own money, is my business. Dat bitch ain't have to cut my face."

Oddly, Matt was in agreement with some of the things Isis was saying. Even he thought it was a little too extreme to go as far as cutting her face wide open. But it wasn't his place to speak about it. Hell, it wasn't even his place to be picking her up from the hospital, because Rita definitely didn't tell him to do so, but like always, Matt had a method to his madness. Everything he did was done with an ulterior motive, so whatever he had in store for Isis, it wasn't going to be beneficial for her.

The highway was pretty much wide open as Rita drove down 1-95, trying to clear her mind. Some people drink, others smoke weed, but with Rita, she liked to drive when she had something on her mind. It was her meditation. It's where she did her best thinking. No distractions, just the open road. No worries about getting jumped or shot at. It was miles away from the hood and all the stress it brings.

There had been so much going on in her life that at times she just felt like fallin' back from the game and never looking back. The only problem she had was the game was all she knew. Driving down the highway, she vividly remembered the times when she was just a little girl and her father, Big Wink, would be in the kitchen cooking at the store. She used to wonder why her dad never came out of the kitchen with any food or why it didn't smell like chicken or fish.

"Daddy, you cookin' in there all day but never have any food to bring out. What you doing in there?" Rita asked.

Big Wink laughed. "I'm doin' grown folk things. I am cooking food, but it isn't for our family's consumption. I give this food to other families."

"So, you're helping other families."

"Exactly. Something like that." Big Wink smiled and patted Rita on her head.

It was funny to Rita, looking back and now realizing he was cooking crack in those Pyrex pots. She never thought in a million years she would be anything like her dad.

Rita wondered if she would have been more like her mother if she hadn't died when Rita was six. Breast cancer took her at a young age, and Rita had little memory of her. It wasn't enough to feel like she knew who her mother was. All she had were pictures and broken memories of her mom.

It was starting to get late, and Rita had to make one more stop before she went back into the neighborhood. She needed to pick up some guns. She had stumbled upon her new gun runner a few months prior.

When White Boy Tom approached her in the club, she thought he was the Feds. He looked just like a narc. Hell, any white man in a black neighborhood would look like a cop.

"Can I buy you a drink?" Tom asked.

Rita looked suspiciously at the white boy standing next to her. "You must think I'm stupid."

"No. Just alone and in need of company."

She rolled her eyes. "You might think a black woman would be flattered by your compliments, but I can assure you, I'm never charmed by the police."

The white boy raised his eyebrows. "You think I'm police?"

"Some sort of law enforcement."

"I can assure you I'm definitely not police or any of the letter boys."

"How can you assure me?" Rita asked.

"Let me buy you a drink and I'll prove it."

Against her better judgement, Rita accepted his offer. The bartender served Rita an orange juice.

"No alcohol?" Tom asked.

"I need to be alert. I don't mess with no drugs or alcohol."

"Cheers to that." He held his glass up to her. They clinked their glasses together and took a sip.

"So, if you're not a cop, what do you do?"

"Let's just say I'm on the other side of the law."

"Oh?"

Tom smiled. "I know what you're thinking, and no, I don't sell drugs."

"I wasn't thinking anything. But if it's not drugs, what is it you do?" She sipped her drink.

"I don't know you well enough to divulge such personal information."

They continued with small talk and getting to know each other.

After a brief pause in the conversation, Tom said, "I need to be honest with you. I know who you are."

"And who am I?"

"You're Big Wink's daughter. And you are expanding your business."

Rita shook her head slowly. "I see." Her senses were on alert. This was some sort of set-up.

"I wanted to get to know you before I offered my services."

"And what might that be?"

"I can get you as much firepower as you need."

Rita smiled. "A gun runner."

"That's me."

After some homework and a few calls, Tom earned a bit of Rita's trust, especially since the first time she bought from him, he took her to his home, where she met his wife and kids. Now, Rita was buying guns just to sell to her workers for a higher price. This way, she could benefit in more than one way. For one, she made a few extra dollars and for two, she really didn't have to worry about her corners getting robbed or her crack houses getting ran in by the stickup boys. Everybody benefited, and at no time would there be a reason to hold onto a gun after a rival shootout. She, as well as her workers, could always throw the guns away and not have to worry about whether they could get another one. Rita was buying between 10 to 15 guns a month, even when she didn't have to.

White Boy Tom waved to Rita from his garage as she pulled into his driveway. He had a nice house in the quieter section of Upper Darby, Pennsylvania, and from the looks of the amount of land he had, the gun business was treating him good. But it wasn't the only thing he had his hands in. Rita knew for sure that he had a meth lab around somewhere.

"Hey, beautiful," he said, seeing Rita getting out of her car and walking toward the garage. "I'm telling you, Rita, if I wasn't married, whoooo I'd make you my wife," he joked, flirting with Rita like he always did.

"Tom, if I was ya wife, you'd probably be broke by now. You know y'all white boys can't handle this good stuff," she shot back. They both laughed at that joke, knowing it had some truth to it. Rita walked into the garage as the door was closing.

Although he only had a few neighbors on that street, he still wanted a little privacy. You never know who's watching. The Feds can be hiding anywhere.

He walked over to the cabinets on the other side of the garage and swung open the door.

"I got something special for you today, little lady," he said, lighting up a cigarette.

"Is that right?" she said, walking over to the cabinet and taking a look inside.

"I got what you may call Ms. Pac-Man. It's a MP-5 submachine gun," he said, grabbing the gun off the shelf. "It has a suppressor with infra-red. It weighs practically nothing, and that's wit' a full 50 clip," he explained, passing her the gun.

Rita was so used to buying handguns that she really didn't have any idea of what she possessed in her hand. This was a new line of artillery that she wasn't even sure she needed. Tom had guns that belonged over in the war in Iraq. The largest common gun she ever had was an AK-47, which was too big for her taste. She ended up trading it for handguns.

"And this, my sweet, is the Sars-308," he said, grabbing the assault rifle hanging on the door. "I call her The Last Air Bender. This bullet can travel through water, wind, fire and earth, and still put a six-inch hole in any two-inch steel door. I guarantee that when you bring her out to play, all the kids will run back into the house," he said, blowing the smoke out of his mouth.

Before Tom could say another word, Rita's phone began to ring. Still holding the MP-5 in one hand, she answered the phone. "Shay, what's good, Mama?" she answered.

"Yo, I need to see you. It's important," Shay said aggressively. "I'm on Fifty-sixth Street right now. Where the hell are you?"

"Damn. What's goin' on?" Rita was concerned by the tone in Shay's voice.

"It's Isis. Dis bitch done lost her fuckin' mind, yo. You gotta get around here ASAP. I'm sitting outside," Shay said then hung up the phone.

Rita took in a deep breath, knowing Isis was probably on some bullshit. It had to be serious because of the way Shay sounded. She stuffed the phone into her back pocket and took another good look at the MP-5. She looked at the Sars-308 in Tom's hand, then looked into the cabinet at the numerous handguns hanging up.

"What are you going to charge me for the Last Air Bender, Ms. Pac-Man, and those twin Glock .40 cals hanging up right there?" she asked, pointing at the cabinet with the MP-5.

"Give me three grand." He quickly calculated the math in his head. "And that's a steal anywhere in America."

***

Dave pulled up to Lump's house and parked on the next street over like he always did. He noticed a familiar car in his driveway that belonged to Ashley, Cees' main girl. He thought nothing of it, until he noticed Ashley coming out of the front door. She wasn't aware that Dave was on the street and watching. Lump and Ashley stood at the door for a brief second, talking about whatever they were talking about, and then Ashley walked off the porch to get into her car, while Lump went back inside the house.

Dave quickly got on his phone and called Lump's cell phone as he watched Ashley walk down the street toward her car, which was parked further down the block. Dave hoped he was just trippin' out and Ashley was dropping Cees off because he was having car problems that morning. For her sake and his, this better had been the case.

"Yo, what's good, playboy," Lump answered, picking up on the third ring.

"Aw, man, I'm chillin'. I was on my way through there to come holla at you about that situation," Dave said, watching Ashley pull off down the street.

"Yeah, that's a good idea. See if you can bring Cees wit' you. I think he should be here too," Lump said, then hung up.

Damn, that's crazy, Dave thought. His hopes for Cees being in the house was impossible. There was no other reason why Ashley should be coming out of Lump's house at 7:00 in the evening. Maybe there was some type of explanation for the visit. Maybe it was nothing. Cees might have sent her over there to pick something up.

All of these thoughts raced through Dave's head. He waited some time to pass before he got out of his car and headed toward Lump's house. One thing for sure was that if she was cheating on Cees with Lump, Cees was definitely going to kill both of them, literally. You could get away with just about anything except when it came down to Ashley, the mother of Cees' only son, whom he'd been with since their teenage years. For her, he was always ready to go the distance with whoever.

"What's good, bro," Lump said, answering the door with nothing but a pair of sweatpants on.

It wasn't looking good off the break, especially since Lump was cut up like a cheap bag of dope. He had muscles everywhere, and it looked like his body was carved by a professional sculptor. This was his main attraction to the women, and it proved to break some of the best housewives, hoodwives, and even a few lesbians.

"*Damn,* it smell like a bitch in here," Dave said, taking a seat on the couch, making that statement to see what kind of reaction he would get from it.

"Yeah, I just got finished smashing the chick from down South Philly I was telling you about," he said, lying about one part, but telling the truth about another.

Dave just sat there and kept his cool, not really wanting to get too involved with the situation. If Cees found out he had anything to do with it, Dave would be just as dead as Lump and Ashley. All Dave wanted to do at that point was get on with the business. This sting was going to be his last one for a while, so he wanted to get it done and out of the way before the shit hit the fan with Cees.

"So, tell me, homie, what's the math on that situation?" Dave inquired, cracking open a Dutch Master and dumping the tobacco out into the large ashtray sitting on the living room table.

"Oh yeah, my man from out West Philly put me on to this chick named Rita who doin' big things out that way. I'ma start doin' my homework on her tomorrow, so I can get a better idea of what we're working wit'. From what I hear, she's worth a nice piece of change, but she's not afraid to squeeze dat trigger either."

Dave just sat there listening to Lump as the weed smoke clouded the air. The last time he heard about a female getting a lot of money in the city was when a chick took over South Philly and was never seen again after escaping federal custody. Half of the time when the rumor was going around that a certain person was getting money, they were never really getting as much as the people said. Dave really hoped that this chick wasn't a waste of his time.

The fire truck sitting on the top of 56th Street was the first thing that caught Rita's attention when she drove down the street. Looking even further, she could see a couple of cop cars posted on the corner and a large crowd of people sitting on the opposite side of the street, where the burning house was being put out. It was Rita's number one crack house, just about burned to the ground.

She was hesitant to park and get out of her car because she had guns that belonged to the United States military in her trunk. Instead, she circled the block and parked around the corner on 57th Street and walked to 56thth Street. When she was within eyesight, Shay walked off from the crowd and met her on the corner.

"What happened to your face?" Rita asked, noticing a dark mark under Shay's eye.

"Nothing. I hit it getting out of bed this morning," she answered, not thinking Rita would have noticed it. "As you can see, the house is gone. The work and the money from the day-shift is gone, and the workers are saying that Isis had something to do with it," Shay explained to Rita.

"Why do they think she had something to do with it?" Rita asked.

"They said that right before the fire, two dudes ran in the house with masks on and robbed it. A woman with a scar on her face was standing on the corner the whole time. Lil John-John said that right before the fire broke out, she disappeared into the alleyway."

"What about you? What do you think?" Rita asked, looking down the street at the unmarked cop car on the corner.

"I don't know. I know that she is well capable of doing it, and I definitely wouldn't put it past her," she said.

Rita flipped out her phone and immediately called Isis's cell phone. If she did have anything to do with this, she was going to get more than a cut across the face this time. She was messing with Rita's gold mine, and until Rita found a new house to sell out of, the money she would be missing would be in the tens of thousands.

Just as she predicted, Isis wasn't answering the phone, and until she had a chance to speak to her, she wasn't going to jump the gun. Rita was good with controlling her temper. It would actually take a lot to get under Rita's skin, but when you finally pushed the right button, she would turn into a monster most people couldn't handle.

"It's funny that I buy guns every month so people won't be able to rob me, and here it is, I'm put out of a house and down today's profit, and not one person got shot behind it," Rita said, looking off into the crowd. "Tell John-John and everybody else standing on that corner to find somewhere else to sell drugs. They can't do it out here anymore. I'm replacing everybody, and I want you to find some workers that's willing to squeeze dat trigger without hesitation," Rita told Shay, turning around and walking off the corner.

She was getting a little agitated about the lack of security and how easy it was for someone to rob her and shut down her crack house in the same night. She had other things on her plate, and she couldn't get too caught up in her feelings about spilled milk. It wasn't about the set-back, but rather the get-back, and if it was anybody who knew how to recover, it would be Rita.

Crack head Mike was the one who answered the door. Sitting at the table in the dining room were Peanut and Fats, two of the workers who were under her a few weeks ago. When Isis first entered the house, it looked as though it was a friendly visit. Seeing a familiar face stopped Peanut from reaching for his gun, which remained on his hip.

Isis was calm and collected as she walked into the house on 60th and Market Street where she used to sell drugs for Rita, carrying a Beretta 9 mm in her hand. She wore a pair of tight blue True Religion jeans, a white wife-beater, and some Air Max sneakers. She had her hair pulled back in a ponytail. Following behind her were Bones and Free, two niggas she'd known most of her life from the hood. They, too, had guns out, and their sole purpose was to shoot anything that moved without Isis's permission. Once Peanut saw their guns drawn, the atmosphere in the room became a little tense, and the visit was no longer considered friendly.

"What's up, Peanut? What's up, Fats?" Isis said, taking a seat on the edge of the table they were sitting at. She clutched the gun in her hand.

"What's all this about?" Fats asked, leaning back in his chair like he was the boss.

"Look, I'm only here to give you guys an opportunity to get down wit' my squad. I know y'all work for Rita, but her days are numbered, and if you knew what was best for you, you would jump on the winning team," Isis offered, remaining in her calm state.

"What makes you think Rita gon' let you run her out? You know how that chick gets busy wit' dat gunplay. If you think I'ma go against her for you, and you can't even back my play, you sadly mistaken. My loyalty is with the one who got the most money and the most guns, and that's not you," Peanut explained.

What he said made all the sense. Isis had a few guns and a couple of goons willing to ride, but she lacked a few key things that could possibly give her success. She didn't have the kind of money Rita had. In fact, she was pretty much broke, nor did she have a drug supplier that would flood her with what she needed. She wanted to break down Rita's whole little operation and take over the streets of West Philly. All she was working with was the rage of getting her face sliced open, which could only get her but so far. She didn't even know for sure whether she wanted to kill Rita, or even if she wanted her dead at all, for that matter.

"You know what? You make a valid point. I guess I should get my money up before trying to start a war," Isis said, looking over at Bones and Free.

Isis stood up to leave, thinking hard about what Peanut just said. As she turned to leave out the front door, a feeling came over her that she never felt before. It felt like the walls were closing in on her and her lungs weren't getting enough air. Her heart started beating fast, and the palms of her hands started to sweat. She felt sweat forming on her scalp. She clutched the 9 mm tightly, spun back around to face Peanut and Fats, and pointed her gun at them.

"What the fuck is you gonna do, rob me now?" Peanut spoke out, placing his hand on the butt of his gun tucked in his waist.

Isis wasn't blind. She could see he was reaching for his gun, but it didn't even matter. Whatever came over her took control of the situation. Her draw was quicker than Peanut's, and by the time he actually got the gun out of his waist, Isis had already fired the first two shots, hitting him in his chest and knocking him out of his chair. She didn't hesitate to keep squeezing the trigger in Fats' direction, knocking a patch out of the side of his head as he was trying to jump behind the table. One of the bullets hit him in his temple, killing him instantly.

Crack head Mike ran down from upstairs to see what was going on, but he was met by a wave of bullets coming from Bones. Mike never saw it coming, and he'd wish he kept his ass upstairs. Several bullets struck him in his chest area, but the fatal shot hit him in his neck, directly in his jugular vein.

Isis was still in the zone. Her adrenaline was flowing. She couldn't believe she'd just shot somebody. She liked the rush. It was like an out-of-body experience as she stared at the dead bodies.

What she did next even shocked Free. Isis went into the kitchen, grabbed a dishrag off the sink, and reached into the freezer. She grabbed a bag of ice she knew would be there, then brought it back into the room. She set the bag of ice directly in the middle of the table as though she was some type of serial killer leaving behind her trademark. She couldn't help but to laugh at her own self. She knew the ice would confuse the hell out of everyone. She stuffed the dish rag into her back pocket and left the house.

As she walked past Bones and Free, she winked and giggled like a little girl. Bones and Free looked at each other on the way out the door. The look that they gave to each other said, "dis bitch is crazy fo' real."

Rita got into her car and was ready to pull off. She scrunched her nose because she smelled like the smoke from the burning house. It was an unwelcome reminder that her main house had just been burned to the ground. She took a deep breath to calm herself. The burnt smell caused her to violently cough. She composed herself and checked the rearview mirror. The unmarked cop car was turning down the street.

Shit, she thought, hoping the car wasn't going to stop by hers. It slowed up and stopped right next to the driver-side door. Two large white men got out of the Crown Victoria, pulling their suit jackets to the side so that their badges were showing. The only thing Rita could think about was the guns she had in her trunk. It was at this time she really wished she'd dropped the guns off at home before coming to see Shay.

The cop on the passenger side was the first to make contact, tapping on the window for Rita to roll it down. She complied, doing her best to play it off like nothing was wrong.

"Can I help you officer?"

"Yeah, sure, Rita. Let me see your license and registration," Detective Mozar asked, catching Rita's attention immediately.

Him knowing her name caught her off guard and for a minute. Rita knew for sure that she was on her way to jail. She played her position and smiled, reaching over into the glove compartment to grab the paperwork. The whole time, both detectives watched her movement closely, hoping they would be able to see something illegal in plain view.

"I'm glad to see Philly's finest taking the time out to learn who their citizens are," she said, passing the paperwork through the window.

"Yeah, we know all of our local drug dealers," the detective shot back. "As a matter of fact, do you mind stepping out of the car so we can search it?"

If Rita didn't know any better, she would have gotten out of the car, but she was somewhat versed with the law concerning illegal searches and seizures. It wasn't that long ago that Rita won a suppression hearing where police violated her Fourth Amendment right by searching her car without a warrant. Her lawyer had explained the whole constitutional right to her in detail, and a lot of it stuck with her.

"Yes, I do have a problem with stepping out of my car and letting you search it. I hope you don't think I'm unaware of my Fourth Amendment constitutional right, do you? You don't have any probable cause to search my car. I'm not giving you consent, nor do you have a warrant," Rita responded, catching the detectives off guard with her knowledge of the law.

Mozar tossed Rita's information back into the car without even looking at it. It never really was his intention to look at it in the first place. He kneeled down next to the driver-side window, resting his arms on the window frame.

"You had a nice little run, Rita. You did ya thing in West Philly, and you might even go down in history being the first female to be successful in the drug game. But, Rita, you might want to consider leaving the drug game alone."

"I don't know where you're getting your info."

"The only reason why you're not going to jail today is because I'm being a nice guy and playing by the rules," Mozar said, cutting her off. I'm quite sure you got something in this car you're not supposed to have," he said, looking back at the trunk. "Look, today, since I'm being such a nice guy, I'm going to give you a pass. But this pass only lasts for today. After today, I'ma stop playing by the rule." He stood up. "Have a nice day." He walked back to the car.

Rita sat there scared to death. Her heart was about to explode through her chest. Not only did she have the guns in the car, but she just remembered that there was some crack in the car she was supposed to be dropping off to Shay. She just sat there in the car and watched the detectives pull off. She didn't even want to drive after that encounter, and after careful thought, she decided to leave the car and walk back around the corner to catch a ride from Shay. Guns and crack together equaled the Feds, and right now, Rita couldn't afford to be dealing with the Feds. They were the hardest law enforcement to beat, and she knew it.

Chapter 3

"Matt! Matt!" Shay yelled from the bedroom.

At first he didn't answer her, because he already had a feeling about what she was calling him for. He came strolling into the room with an angry look on his face like Shay was bothering him. It was his way of counteracting the upcoming argument he knew was bound to happen.

"What's up?" he said, standing in the doorway, picking food out of his teeth.

"Yo, I'm light two and a half ounces of powder and five hundred dollars," Shay said, looking at the remaining cocaine and money sitting on the dresser.

Shay and Matt been together for a couple of years now, but they always kept their business and personal life separated on the strength that the relationship worked out better that way. Shay had her own money and Matt had his, and the only time they ever shared was when it was totally necessary. For the past month or so, Shay had noticed that the money and drugs in her stash was coming up short sometimes. At first she didn't think anything of it, until it happened more than once. Then she got suspicious. This particular time was actually the third, and the amount which was missing was more than usual.

"What you telling me for? What, you think I took it?"

"Nigga, unless you got somebody else living here, the only other person that could have touched my shit is you. If you needed something from me, you should've just asked me."

"Hold up, bitch. Don't get beside yaself," he said, pointing at her as he walked across the room. "I run shit up in dis house, and whatever is up in here is mine."

Shay couldn't believe what she was hearing coming out of his mouth. Then again, she could believe it considering his actions for the past few weeks. Shay knew for sure that he was either fucking somebody else or using some type of drug. It was times when his dick wouldn't even get hard, even if Shay decided to give him some head. Any woman's antenna would go up asap.

"And I swear I hope you're not putting dis shit up ya nose again," she said, pointing at the cocaine.

"Asked you, huh? I shouldn't have to ask you for shit. What's mine is yours and what's yours is mine," Matt shot back. "And whatever I decide to put up my fuckin' nose is my fucking business."

Shay looked at him in disgust. She didn't want to say anything out of the love she had for him, but it was times Shay could see the cocaine sweating out of his pores. "Fuckin' coke head," she mumbled under her breath, but not low enough for Matt not to hear her.

"Fuck did you just call me?" he snapped back, walking up closer to her.

"Nothin', man. Just don't touch my shit please," Shay said, becoming a little scared of the aggression Matt was starting to show.

She couldn't get another word out before Matt smacked fire out of her mouth. He hit her so hard, Shay could taste the blood in her mouth. He grabbed her by the hair and lifted her up to her feet. Still kind of dazed, Shay tried to fight back, swinging punches in every direction. She knocked over the lamp sitting on the dresser, and only wished that she could have grabbed it to bust Matt upside the head with it.

Using his strength to pin her arms against her sides, Matt lifted Shay off of her feet and slammed her onto the bed. He wrapped both of his hands around her neck and began choking her, periodically loosening his grip so that he could punch her in the ribs. Shay thought that Matt was going to kill her this time. He never really went this far before. He was actually choking her until she was damn near passed out.

"I run shit around here," he repeatedly said, yanking off pieces of her clothing. "Everything in this house is mine, including you."

Shay was tired, and her ribs were hurting. She could hardly catch her breath, let alone try to fight him off of her. She watched as he peeled off her clothes, and before she could tell him to stop, the warmth of his mouth was all over her pussy. He released her hands that he had pinned down, and wrapped his arms around her thighs, shoving his warm, wet tongue deep within her womb.

"Please stop," she begged, confused about the mixed feelings she was having about what was going on.

He just got finished beating her ass, and now he wanted to eat her pussy. Shay knew it was wrong, and in fact, she was well aware that he was raping her, because she definitely didn't want to have sex right now, but in some odd way, she was starting to enjoy the feeling of his mouth. She tried her best to squirm out of his grasp, pushing down on his head. Again, she pleaded for him to stop, but he didn't. He only gripped her tighter.

"I told you, everything in this house is mine, even you." He climbed on top of Shay.

He tried to kiss her, but she turned her head to the side before his lips could touch hers. He wasted no time slamming his large dick inside of her, forcing himself past her unwanted point of entrance. It hurt Shay's pussy feeling Matt's dick pushing in and out of her with brute force, but the physical pain she was feeling could never equal up to the mental pain she felt. She just lay there while Matt fucked her like she was trash.

Dave, Lump, and Cees sat in the bar, throwing back a couple of drinks as they discussed business. Lump had been doing his homework on Rita, and thus far, he was breaking down the information he accumulated in the past couple of days.

"She's hard to pin down." Lump took a sip of his Hennessy.

"What you mean by that?" Dave asked.

"She's smart. Like, real smart. She's got eyes and ears everywhere. I've tried to follow her, and she loses me every time. I don't know if she sees me or not, but she makes so many turns that I can't keep following or she'll definitely know I'm there."

Cees snorted. "We've gotten to other niggas who were supposedly smart. She a bitch. It ain't no thing."

Lump shook his head. "No, I'm telling you, she's different. Like, I got to be real careful who I talk to about her. Other niggas have tried our same play about a year ago."

"But they ain't us," Cees said.

"Let him speak," Dave said.

"She knew about the plan before it happened," Lump said. "She's got a lot of respect in the hood, and when she put the word out, those niggas were never seen again."

"I say fuck it. Let her know we're following her and let's get this bitch. I'm ready to enjoy some time off."

"It ain't that simple. She's got niggas surrounding her all the time. And they ain't there for fun and games. Them niggas is ready to throw down."

Dave was staring into his drink. "So, what you think we should do?"

"I'm probably going to need a couple more days to get it right, but as soon as I get the information I'm looking for, we'll be good to go," Lump said, throwing back his final shot. "I would love to stay and play, but I got to get back to work. I'ma call y'all tomorrow to let you know what's going on." He gave them daps and walked out.

Dave and Cees stayed in the bar, not yet ready to leave. Cees ordered another round, turning his normal single shot into a double. Dave could see that it was obviously something on his mind.

"Damn, Cannon, why the long face?" Dave tapped Cees on the arm, snapping him out of his daze.

Cees looked at Dave with a hurtful look in his eyes that Dave never saw before. He'd known Cees for every bit of ten years and not once did he ever see him like this. Cees didn't really want to bother Dave with his problems, but he was sick.

"Yo, I think Ashley's stepping out on me," Cees said, throwing back the double shot.

"Damn, Cees, don't you think that's a little extreme? What makes you think she's going that far?"

"Man, I just got this gut feeling something ain't right. She's dressing up and going out more, leaving my son over her mom's house for hours at a time. She came in the house a couple nights ago around 11:30, and she had this look on her face like she was guilty of something."

"C'mon, man, you might be overreacting. You and I both know that girl loves you more than anything in the world," Dave said, trying to make Cees feel better.

"Right before I left the house to come here, she was getting dressed up to go out. I asked her where she was going, and she told me over her sister's house."

"Well, what's wrong wit' dat?"

"She never put on high heels and a skirt to go over her sister's house. I just looked at her, then put my head down."

Dave was almost tempted to tell Cees that Ashley was probably on her way to meet up wit' Lump. He could tell by the way Lump rushed out of there that it had to be a shot of pussy waiting somewhere for him. Dave really didn't want nothing to do with none of this. He knew that the end result was going to be ugly, so before Cees could go on about his problems, Dave changed the mood.

"Yo, you know what you need?" Dave said, throwing his final shot back before getting up.

"What's that"?

"You and Ashley need to take a good vacation after this next sting. Y'all just need some time away together. That would be good for the both of you. And you know what else you need?"

"Tell me," Cees said, looking for something to uplift his spirits.

"You need to hit the strip club, my man. It's time we make it rain, baby boy," Dave announced with a big smile on his face, but on the inside really feeling sad for his friend. "It's time to make it rain."

Ironically, Shay and Matt walked into the pool hall together, despite the event that happened earlier. The pool hall was the place to go whenever Rita called a meeting, and considering the fact that Peanut and Fats was killed last night, this meeting definitely needed to happen. Too much had been going on, and before Rita would let her small organization go down the drain, she'd rectify, clarify, and establish new order.

About eight people showed up for the meeting. Rita, Shay, Matt, and one person from each corner Rita owned, which was about five, were there. They all gathered around one of the pool tables in the back of the hall, and the first order of business was trying to figure out what happened to Peanut and Fats. The reason why Shay had another mark on her face would have to wait until later. Rita had spotted the bruise the moment Shay walked through the door, and the stupid look they both had on their faces was suspicious enough for Rita to want to inquire about it a little bit later.

"Before I continue, I want you to make sure Peanut and Fats' funeral is paid for. I don't want their mother paying for nothing. I don't care how much it cost," Rita told Shay off the break. "Now, I called this meeting because a lot of shit's been going on, and I want some answers. First, did anybody hear anything about Peanut and Fats?" Shay asked, hitting the cue-ball up against the wall of the table.

Chris, the person who was supposed to work the shift right after Peanut and Fats, was the first person to speak. "When I came to the block, the cops was already there. Shelly said she was the one who found the bodies."

"Who is Shelly?" Rita asked.

"Shelly is one of the normal crackheads around there. She said that Peanut was shot in his chest and Fats was shot in the head. Smoke Mike was in the house too, and he got shot over four times."

"So, don't nobody know who did it?" Shay chimed in.

"Naw, but I think I got an idea who did it, and I'm almost sure it was her."

"Who?" Shay asked with a curious look on her face, looking over at Rita, who had the same look on hers.

"I think it was Isis. Shelly said that when she walked into the house and saw the bodies on the ground, one of the things she couldn't help but to notice was a large bag of ice sitting in the middle of the table by itself. I be around Isis every day, and I swear that shit sounds like something she would do."

Everybody got quiet, thinking about Isis's capabilities. She didn't come off to be a killer in Shay's eyes, but for Rita, she wouldn't put it past her. Shay didn't know her cousin Isis like Rita did, and if Isis was anything like her father, Rita knew she could have a potential problem on her hands.

"I think we should try to find out where Isis is," Rita said, wanting to do more than just question her about the murders.

If she did kill Peanut and Fats, she's probably going to be coming after me sometime in the future, Rita thought. It would be tragic for Rita to have to explain to their grandma that Isis was dead, and it would be an even more tragic event explaining Rita's death. So, before a crowd of people would be crying over Rita's casket, singing sad songs, Isis and whoever else was rolling with her would become target practice.

As the meeting continued in the back of the pool hall, the front door swung open and in walked Isis, Bones, Free, and Banks, a new addition to her squad. Everybody had guns out, and wasn't nobody doin' any talking as they began spreading the floor.

The meeting was going on so far in the back of the pool hall that Rita didn't even notice what was going on up front. The music blasting from the jukebox didn't make anything any better. The manager stationed in a booth beside the front door felt something big was about to go down.

"Yo, I don't think you have to look any further for Isis," Chris said, being the first to notice Isis walking up with a gun in her hand. "She's right there," he said, pulling his gun from his waist.

Everybody turned to look at the same time the loud music shut off, leaving nothing but the sound of Isis's Beretta 9 mm roaring through the air. Other people who were in the pool hall all took cover or ran out the front door. Several bullets knocked holes into the pool table Rita and her crew stood around. Bullets were chipping ivory off of the pool balls on the table. Everybody scattered, trying to find something to take cover behind.

Dre, one of Rita's boys, noticed Banks and Free creeping up from the side with their guns raised, looking for a target. "You got two coming up from the side," Dre yelled out, warning everybody about the ambush.

Rita, Shay, Chris, and Matt all pulled out their guns, returning fire in Isis's direction, making her retreat behind one of the vending machines. Dre began emptying his .357 Mag at Free, but he took a bullet in his arm from Banks bringing up the rear.

Bones jumped on top of one of the pool tables to get a better view of where everybody was at. He saw Matt trying to dart across the room and threw four shots in his direction, knocking chips of wood off the tables following behind him.

Rita lay on the ground, looking under the table for some legs to shoot at. Isis was doing the same thing, and when she saw Rita, she fired a single shot at her, hitting the leg of the table, missing Rita's head by only two inches.

It was almost simultaneously that the sounds of gunfire stopped in the pool hall. Just about out of bullets, Isis, Bones, Free, and Banks backed out of the pool hall, just as smooth as they came in. Shay started to run after them, but Rita grabbed her by the arm, stopping her in case they would be waiting for somebody to come out the front door.

"Is everybody good?" Rita yelled out to her crew. She slowly got up from the floor.

"I'm hit, but I'm good," Dre answered, holding his arm where the bullet hit him.

"We gotta get out of here before the cops come," Matt warned, seeing the manager on the phone.

Rita took the lead role in checking the front door to see if Isis had left or if they were still out there waiting. She approached the door carefully with her gun still out. When she got to the door, she could see a couple of cars speeding out of the parking lot. Nobody else was in sight, so it was clear for them to get out.

Everybody darted out of the pool hall and went straight for their cars. Chris and his boy got into his car, Rita and her shooter got into hers, Matt and Shay peeled off, and Dre was leaving with the rest of the crew.

"Don't go to the hospital," Rita yelled out to Dre before he pulled off. "I got somebody to take care of that. Just follow me," she told him while pulling off.

It wasn't a question whether or not Isis was behind the bullshit. She wasn't faking when she came into the pool hall, and if Rita wasn't surrounded by angels that night, her brains would have painted the pool hall floor. As Rita drove down the street, she realized what needed to be done. One thing that was for sure was that Isis wasn't playing any games wit' Rita. The cut running down her face was beyond personal, and for a moment, Rita regretted not just killing Isis instead of giving her a pass with the buck-fifty.

"Yeah, what's good," Rita said, answering her phone after noticing that it was Shay.

"I guess this mean we're at war?" Shay asked Rita, looking over at the blood on Matt's jeans.

"No, we're far from being at war with Isis. She's nobody, and I'll be dammed if I waste time and money running around the city playing cowboys and Indians wit' dis bitch. You let me deal wit' Isis, and as far as everything else is concerned, it's business as usual," Rita commanded in a calm tone, looking off into the road ahead of her. "Just tighten up the security a little for the next couple of days," she said, and then hung up the phone.

Chapter 4

It was already one o'clock in the morning, and Ashley still wasn't home. This was the first time she stayed out this late, and it burned Cees up with every minute that went by. He sat outside on the front porch, waiting, hoping that he could catch her being dropped off by whoever she was with. Somebody had to drop her off being as though her car was in the driveway and had been there ever since Cees came home about three hours ago.

Weed mixed with a little bit of Hennessy equaled the Glock .40-cal sitting in his lap and the desire to use it in the event Ashley was with a nigga. He couldn't help but wonder where he was going wrong and what he was doing to make his girl look for happiness somewhere else. The streets was a part of his life, and ever since he could remember, Ashley accepted it and enjoyed the benefits of the fast money.

The sound of a pair of high heels clicking down the sidewalk caught Cees' attention as he inhaled a deep drag of the cush. He almost choked when he realized it was Ashley, walking up with the skankiest outfit on he'd ever seen her wear. She wore a pair of mini shorts, some open-toe stilettos with the straps, and a tight-fitted, cropped Ed Hardy t-shirt that exposed her belly. Cees was sitting just looking at her, resembling a whore.

Ashley didn't even see Cees sitting on the porch when she walked up, searching in her pocketbook for her keys.

She got to the top of the steps and was startled to see Cees sitting there.

"I see you had a busy night," Cees said, grabbing the gun from off of his lap. "Sit down," he directed, pointing with the gun to the empty seat next to him.

She sat down but was scared as hell seeing the look on his face, along with the gun in his hand. She pretty much had an idea of the conversation that was about to take place, so every answer she gave to the questions that were asked needed to be swift and accurate to avoid any detection of a lie.

"Look, I really don't know what I did to you or what I'm not doing for you, but I'm sorry. Whatever the problem is, I can fix it if you give me the chance. I just need you to help me understand where I'm going wrong."

The opening of the conversation caught Ashley by surprise. She knew for certain that Cees was about to ask her where she'd been, who she'd been with, why she didn't call, and how she got home, but none of those questions took place.

"There's nothing goin' on, boo. I just went out wit' the girls tonight, and I lost track of time. I was—"

"Ashley! Ashley! Stop!" Cees said, cutting her off. "Can you actually sit here and try to convince me that there's nothing going on? Do you actually think I don't know when there's something wrong wit' you? I practically raised you, so don't sit here and insult my intelligence like I'm the average Joe nigga on the streets, especially when I know you better than you know your own self."

"Can we talk about this tomorrow?" Ashley asked, not very willing to say something that she might regret.

"Naw, we can talk about it right now," Cees demanded, tuning to face Ashley.

She had her whole game plan laid out for when she walked in the house, but Cees was throwing a monkey-wrench into the game that she didn't expect. Ashley was so green to what was going on, she didn't realize that every question she thought he was going to ask her had been answered already. She was stuck. She knew that it wasn't any excuse she could use to justify her coming in the house at one o'clock in the morning, and on top of that, she wasn't even driving her car. Cees wasn't stupid, and before the night was over, Ashley was going to reveal all her dirty little secrets.

Isis and Banks met Basco at the recreation center on 46th and Brown Street. Banks used to deal with Basco on small scale drug buys, and he set up the meeting for Isis to score some coke and hopefully get in his good graces for a possible front. Her money wasn't up to the level of Rita's, but she wasn't broke either. She had enough to buy half a brick, just as long as it wouldn't cost no more than 9 grand. That's all she really needed to get on, and now that she had her own little corner in Southwest Philly, it wouldn't be hard for her to turn that little 18 ounces into a brick, then a brick into two.

When she pulled up to the rec center, she couldn't help but notice a number of guys standing outside of Basco's white Cadillac Escalade. He was sitting in the passenger seat with the door open, laughing and joking with his boys. All the laughter stopped once Isis and Banks walked up to the truck.

"Basco, what's good wit' you, big homie?" Banks said, breaking the small amount of tension building up from Basco's boys.

"Damn, Banks, I didn't think you was going to come. I was damn near getting ready to leave if you didn't show up in the next five minutes."

"My bad, Basco, but look, this is the person I was telling you about." He pointed to Isis.

Basco took a good look at Isis, immediately noticing the long scar running down her face. She looked cute standing there in a pair of blue Dereon jeans, some spaghetti-strapped sandals, and a white tank-top. Her long hair was pulled back into a ponytail, and in her hand was a Roberto Cavalli tote bag. Even with the cut on her face, she still managed to look good.

"A pretty girl thug. I like that," Basco said, checking Isis out. "C'mon, get in the truck."

Isis complied, hopping in the back seat with Banks. Basco just closed the door and sat in the passenger seat, not really needing to go anywhere, because business could have been done right there. One of his boys got in the driver side, while the other stood outside of the door.

"So, what can I do for you today, li'l mama?" Basco asked, staring out of the window.

"Well, I'm trying to buy some work from you, but I also wanted to discuss some other business wit' you as well," Isis stated.

"How much work are you talking about?"

"I got nine grand right now. I was trying to get a half."

"Nine grand? I don't even answer my phone for nine grand. I don't know what Banks told you about me, but you might be barking up the wrong tree, li'l mama. If you want to fuck wit' the big dogs, you gotta get ya money straight," Basco said, looking in the rearview mirror at Isis.

Isis was starting to feel some type of way about the way Basco was trying to brush her off. To her, nine grand was a lot of money considering that's all she had. Basco was a little arrogant, but he was cocaine-rich, which meant that he could talk as much slick shit out of his mouth as he wanted to.

"Get out," Isis told Banks with an attitude, who was still sitting next to her in the back seat.

He didn't think twice about doing what she said, not knowing what she was about to do. Basco looked at his boy, making sure that he was on point. He was confused about what was going on and why Isis dismissed Banks so aggressively.

"You see, Basco, I'm not sure what Banks told you about me, so let me tell you this. I may not be rich in money, but I'm damn sure wealthy with fear and respect. With that being said, the reason why I came to you is because I'm looking for a sponsor. Someone who can supply me with good cocaine for a reasonable price. I got nine grand, so if you can match what I buy for the next couple of flips, I guarantee you'll be answering ya phone when I call."

Basco looked at his boy, thinking about what Isis was talking about. She had a good game, and Basco was feeling the scar on her face, but it was going to take a hell of a lot more than that to get Basco to front her some coke, especially since he didn't even know her. He looked in his rearview again, checking Isis out, letting his mind wander in places it had no business.

"Get out," Basco told his boy, then directed Isis to come up to the front seat. "You see, li'l mama, I'm not just rich in money, but I'm also wealthy in fear and respect too. I think that if you're willing, we can work something out," he said with a seductive look in his eyes, staring at her thick thighs and fat ass as she climbed into the driver seat.

"What did you have in mind?" Isis asked, already see-ing through Basco like glass.

Like any man with a dick, Isis knew that at the end of the day, he probably wanted a shot of pussy in exchange for his business. Basco was a fat, black-ass nigga who looked like the only way he could get some pussy from a bad chick was if he paid for it. A vicious trick. He wasn't even a cute fat boy. He was ugly as hell, and just the thought of him sweating overtop of Isis almost made her gag.

"So, you're sitting here telling me that you're not going to tell me his name?" Cees asked, pouring himself a shot of Hennessy from the bar.

"I'm not going to tell you his name, Cees, so please stop asking me," Ashley answered, tired and ready to go to bed.

Cees and Ashley never got a chance to make it to the bedroom the night before. They'd been downstairs argu-ing and fighting for the past six hours, venting, getting everything out on the table about what was going on. Ashley couldn't live a constant lie. She'd been wanting to stop cheating on Cees for a while now, but she got so caught up that it became hard to stop. It wasn't that she had any feelings for the person she was cheating with, nor the one and only time she had sex with him, but it was more so the fun she was enjoying while she was with him. It was like he brought her alive after she'd been hidden from the world for so long.

"We need to work through this," Cees said.

"Look, you already know what happened. I slept with him once. I like the way he makes me feel when we're together. I've been locked up in this house with the bay while you galivant around the streets doing God knows what with God knows who. I'm tired of it. I want to feel whole again, and he makes me feel wanted, respected, and valued."

"I make you feel those things."

"No, you don't, Cees. I know you've cheated on me. Too many times to count. Even though I'm not out in the streets like you, people talk. I hear about all of it. How do you think that makes me feel?" She took a deep breath. "It's embarrassing to hear that you're at the strip club, fucking strippers, spending all of our money that could be for our baby."

"But—"

She stopped him immediately. "No *buts*, Cees. Then when you get home, you don't pay attention to me or the baby. You watch TV, you smoke a blunt and drink until you pass out on the couch. I need to be valued. Do you get it?"

Cees was stunned that Ashley had these feelings. He thought that since he was giving her money, she was happy. It never occurred to him to think how his actions affected the people around him. "Wow. I never knew you felt this way."

"Of course you didn't know. You never ask about me. You never have any conversations with me about how I'm feeling or what I'm thinking. It's always about you and your problems."

Cees didn't know how to respond. She was right, and she called him out. It was times during the argument that Cees wished she'd just lied to him instead of telling him the truth. He wasn't ready. Ashley wasn't ready, but as soon as she got the chance, she exposed Cees and his faults as well.

"So, now what?" Ashley asked, breaking the silence in the room, wanting nothing more than to put it all behind them.

It was unequivocal that Ashley loved Cees and wanted things to be better for both of them and for their son, but she knew that if she told Cees who she'd been messing around with, he was going to kill him, hands down. That's the only reason why he wanted to know his name so bad. She knew Cees all too well to be foolish enough to fall for that. If he wanted a name, he'd have to find that out on his own. Ashley didn't want another person's death on her hands, and being honest with herself, the guy wasn't even worth killing because he meant nothing.

Cees just stood there with his head down, not knowing the answer to the question she'd just asked. It wasn't something he could answer right away, and Ashley not telling him who she was messing with wasn't making it any better. His insecurities came to the surface. He wasn't the big dog, perfect man, head of the house he thought he was. It even left him wondering if his son was really his.

Isis left the hotel room feeling disgusted with herself for giving Basco a shot of pussy. It was definitely the worst sex she'd ever had in her whole entire life. Not only was he fat and nasty, but his dick was small, and he didn't know how to eat pussy. He kept grunting and making stupid noises, and it was at one point, Isis looked over at his clothes on the ground and could see shit stains in his boxers. It made her gag.

The only good thing that came out of this ordeal was that Isis was leaving the hotel with a whole brick. It wasn't for free, and she damn sure worked hard for it, considering the horrible sexual encounter. She gave up the nine grand and now owed Basco seven grand for the brick. It was a sacrifice she had to make for the better, and it was definitely going to be a one-time thing. She wouldn't fuck Basco again if he gave her a brick for free.

Isis had a new block on 56th and Greenway Avenue, and for now, she was only thinking about getting her money up. The beef with Rita was still on, but at the same time, she had to establish her own path. She couldn't waste time running around in a war with Rita without having any money to fall back on, and even though Isis had a couple of goons running with her, Rita had a small army.

As she was driving through the city on her way to meet up with Free and Bone, her phone started to ring. She knew it was Matt from the moment she looked at her phone. At first, she wasn't going to answer it, feeling like there was nothing to talk about after she just got finished shooting at him, but after the fourth ring, she said, what the hell.

"What are you calling my phone for?" Isis answered with an attitude.

"Damn, you shoot me in the leg and damn near killed me, and this is all I get when I call you," Matt joked. "I thought me and you was better than that."

"C'mon, Matt, you can't keep playing both sides of the field. It just don't look right, plus you can end up getting yaself hurt."

A lot of people didn't know about the relationship Isis and Matt had. They had a little history together back in the day, before Shay stole him away from Isis. Even during the time Matt and Shay was together, they still remained sexual, even till this day. There wasn't too much love involved, as it was the sexual chemistry they had with each other, but even with that, it maintained a certain bond only the two of them shared.

"You know Shay's going to kill you if she found out that you're calling me," she joked back. "So, what do you want? I really don't have time to be playing around with you, Matt," she said, now becoming serious.

"I just wanted to check up on you to make sure you was all right. See if you needed anything, you know."

"Thanks for asking, Matt, but I'm good. I don't need nothing but a nice hot bath and a bottle of Patron," she said, thinking about Basco's sweat dripping all over her.

"Can I come see you?" he asked, hoping she would say yeah.

Isis thought about it. She had mixed feelings about seeing Matt. She knew exactly how this visit was going to end up if she said yeah come on, and being as though she just got finished fucking Basco, she really wasn't in the mood for no more dick for today. Then again, she could have used a good sexual experience to do away with the last one. At least, that's what she thought to herself.

"I gotta pass you up today. I'm going through some-thing right now, but I'll call you back if anything changes," Isis said, then hung up the phone.

Matt was cool and all, but as far as Isis was concerned, he really couldn't be trusted as long as he remained on the opposite side of the fence. At the same time, she wanted to keep him on call, just to stay on top of what Rita was up to. He was good for some things, and Isis was going to make good use of him as much as she could.

"How much information do we have on Sarita Powell?" Detective Mozar asked his partner, Detective Seal.

They'd been investigating Rita for a few months, and throughout the past month, Mozar noticed an increase in crime in the neighborhood she roamed, including a recent double homicide in a crack house he believe she owned. They tried their best to build up enough evidence against her that would hold up in court, but every time they thought they had something, Rita slipped out of their grasp. It irritated the detectives because they knew she was the ringleader of her crew. She stayed under the radar so good that there were people in her own organization that didn't even know she was the boss.

"We don't have too much of nothing, and I think we better start moving fast before the FBI get involved. The captain said they called last week, inquiring about her from an anonymous tip coming from somebody in her crew."

"The Feds. Shit." Mozar was tired of them stealing cases after they'd put in the hard work.

Putting Rita behind bars was Mozar's main focus. Catching her in the act of a crime was the hard part. Every informant the detectives sent her way came back empty handed. It was like she knew not to deal with them. Mozar was running out of patience, but not out of ideas. After hearing the Feds got an anonymous tip from somebody in her organization, the best thing to do at this point would be to find out who the weakest link was. If it took shaking down every corner she owned, that's what Mozar was willing to do. In fact, he was willing to do that and more. His methods of shaking down were far from legal.

Everybody went to Peanut's funeral. It had to be over one hundred people on their way to the church on 54th and Catherine Street. He wasn't just some average nigga in the streets people didn't care about. He was somebody, and a lot of people loved him. He left behind two kids, a two-month-old baby boy and a four-year-old little girl. It was a tough blow for a lot of people to hear about his death and how he had died. Isis didn't have the slightest idea what she had done and how many people she hurt.

This is how it was in the city of Philadelphia on a daily basis. The young ran around all day, killing each other for just about any reason they could come up with. It became like a fad to get a body under your belt or to be known for vicious shoot-outs. Boys thought they would become a man the moment they pulled the trigger for the first time, and little girls thought they became women after they lost their virginity. The hood was all messed up, and it was days like today that reality sank in about how messed up the youth really were.

Cars lined up, back to back to back, and as the hearse drove through the neighborhood on its way to the church, the sounds of honking horns filled the air. Shay and Rita drove in the same car, following behind Peanut's mother. Paying for the funeral was a far cry from making anything better, but Rita made sure that he had the best. In all, the cost was around 10k, and that wasn't including flowers. His casket alone cost 4k and his suit was tailor made by Prada. Money didn't mean a thing to Rita, and in two days, she was ready to do the same thing for Fats.

The hood wasn't the only people at the funeral. Detective Mozar was there too, getting a good look at every thug that walked into the church to pay their respects. It was not surprising that shootouts occurred at funerals, especially when rival crews beef and the person that did the murdering was still at large. The one thing Rita made sure of was that security was at an all-time high, and that security wasn't from the police. If Isis was stupid enough to try to shoot up the funeral, Rita had goons posted up both in and outside of every part of the church. To most people, it would be more than disrespect to have a shootout at a church during the funeral, but for the people who lived by the street rule, gunplay at a wake was all fair game in war.

Hopefully, today would be one of those days that nothing else took place but the remembering of man who lost his life to a senseless crime. Hopefully, today the thugs in the streets could learn something. Hopefully, today the people would look at Marcel Grant as a good man and a good father, and not as Peanut, the neighborhood drug dealer.

Chapter 5

With the recession going and the police department taking a hit with all the budget cuts, Mozar was becoming just as bad as the people he was locking up. He sat on 60th and Arch Street, watching all the traffic going in and out of Rita's crack house. This was one of the spots he'd busted before, but he never got a chance to make a proper arrest, because Rita's worker got rid of the cocaine when Mozar and his narcotics team rushed the house. They busted through the doors, screaming, "Police! Put your hands up!"

Mozar ran up the stairs. He knew he only had a finite amount of time before they would get rid of the coke. He needed the evidence to solidify the bust. It's hard to retrieve evidence that's dissolving in acid.

He hadn't considered they'd be so sophisticated to use acid. He thought they would try to flush it down the toilet. He got to the top of the steps and burst into the room. "Hands up!" he yelled.

The workers stepped away from the trash cans on the table. Mazar quickly grabbed one of the cans. He looked inside. "No!" He saw the last remnants of coke dissolving in the acid. He knocked all the cans off the table. "Fuck!" His bust was busted.

Today, Mozar was riding solo. He wasn't trying to make a bust, nor arrest anybody, for that matter. In fact, he wasn't even in a police car. For what he was about to do, he didn't want to draw any attention to himself unless it was totally necessary.

He sat and waited until finally Shay showed up at the house, parking her Dodge Charger at the end of the block and walking down the street toward the house. Mozar quickly pulled off from his spot, hoping he would be able to catch her before she got back to her car.

Shay took a good look around before she walked up the steps and into the crack house. She had a small trash bag in one hand, while her other hand rested on the gun sitting on her waist. She was picking up a couple of grand and dropping off some product for the night shift, something she did every evening of the week, around 7:30, right when the sun was about down.

The transaction lasted every bit of two minutes, and Shay was on her way back out the door, headed for her car. On point, she noticed a car parked behind hers that wasn't there when she went into the house. The old Delta 88 with tinted windows didn't look like a cop car at all. These were the kind of squatters young thugs rolled around in, doing stick-ups.

Shay discreetly pulled the gun off her waist and held it to her side as she walked to the driver-side door to her car. Before she could open it, the driver-side door of the car behind her opened up. She gripped the gun tighter, using her thumb to take the safety off.

Mozar stepped out of the car with his police badge in one hand and the other resting on the gun sitting in his holster. Once Shay saw that it was a white man getting out of the car, she knew it wasn't about to be a stick-up. The police badge caught Shay's attention immediately. She tried to tuck the gun into her back pocket, but as she did, Mozar noticed it. He pulled his gun out of his holster and pointed it right at her.

"Drop the gun and get down on ya knees," he said in a low voice, trying not to catch the attention of the crackheads walking up and down the street.

Shay did exactly what he said, thinking that she was going to jail. She'd hoped that somebody would see her and run to the house to tell the workers to get rid of the coke she just dropped off. Mozar leaned over and grabbed her gun off the ground, along with her Prada tote bag. Shay just sat there on her knees, watching as Mozar went through her pocketbook.

"Is this a shakedown or are you going to actually arrest me?" she asked, looking around at the lack of back-up he had with him. Normally, cops would have been swarming the place if it was a raid, but something told Shay this wasn't a raid.

"Get up," Mozar said, taking the wad of money out of her bag, then throwing it at her. "Now, you got two choices. You can get in ya car and pull off and act like this never happened, or I can lock you up for carrying a gun and possession with intent to deliver."

"What do you mean 'possession with intent to deliver'? I didn't have any drugs on me," Shay said with a confused look on her face.

Mozar reached into his pocket and pulled out a small plastic bag. There had to be about 21 grams of crack bagged up in 5 by 5 baggies. He dangled it around in the air before tossing it onto the hood of her car.

"Like I said, you got a choice to make," Mozar said, placing his gun back into his holster.

This was a real live shakedown. Shay never experienced nothing like this before and was shocked at how it was going down. She had five grand in her bag, which was now in Mozar's pocket, and a choice to either go home or go to jail. Now wasn't the time to be playing any games with her life. It was a no brainer. She could always get the money back, and it would probably cost more to go to jail, bail out, and pay a lawyer to fight the case.

"If you needed money, I could have easily put you on the payroll," Shay said, grinning as she opened her car door.

"Tell ya friend Rita that the longer she sells drugs in my city, the more I'm going to tax her," he said, walking up to the driver-side door and tossing Shay's clip-less gun onto her lap.

"Well, speaking for Rita, the offer still stands if you wanna come work for us. Believe me, the pay is way better than what you just took off of me," she said, putting the car in drive. "Think about it and get back wit' me. I'm sure you already know how to find me."

Mozar started to say something, but then kept his mouth shut. The idea actually didn't sound that bad, considering the fact that he would make triple what he made on the force. But Mozar wasn't in it just for the money. He wanted to establish dominance over not only the streets, but also over the police department he was getting so tired of working for. If that meant playing dirty, both in and outside of the uniform, then Mozar was more than willing to entertain to the idea.

Isis pulled up to the school where Basco told her to meet him. He thought that he was going to get lucky and get another shot of pussy from Isis in exchange for some more coke. He doubted that she was going to come correct with the money that she owed him from the last score, but he was wrong. Isis jumped in the truck, and the first thing she pulled out of her bag was the money she owed him, counting it out in front of him like it was nothing. Her block was doing pretty good, and at this point, she really didn't need any more handouts, especially from somebody like Basco.

"I take it that you got all my money," he said, looking over at Isis counting.

"Yeah, and if you can sell me a brick for seventeen K right now, I'll buy it from you," she said, passing him the seven grand she owed him, then continued counting.

"Seventeen K?" Basco asked arrogantly. "I guess the hotel is on me tonight," he said, leaning over and putting his hand on Isis's thigh.

She almost threw up just thinking about the shit stains in his underwear. She almost had the urge to pull the .38 snub from her back pocket and shoot Basco in the head for even attempting to ask her for some pussy. At this point, it was kind of disrespectful, seeing as how she was coming with money.

"Naw, Basco, that was a one-shot deal," she said, pushing his hand off of her thigh. "But what I can do is tell you that I got word that a certain person plans on robbing you. I think that information alone should be worth the price of admission."

"Rob me? Who da fuck's gonna be stupid enough to try and rob me? I'm muthafuckin' Basco," he said, raising his voice.

"Look, seventeen K or I can go to someone else," she said, reaching for the doorknob.

Basco wasn't just some average nigga in the hood, so when he heard Isis talking like that, it made him upset. Maybe she was right. Maybe the information she had was worth the price of admission. One thing was for sure; Basco wasn't willing to take any chances passing up this kind of information, even if it cost him a little. Who, what, when, where and how, this kind of info was going to have to wait until later. Right now, Basco really just wanted to focus on the actual robber, wanting nothing more than to make an example out of him or anybody else that wanted to pull this kind of stunt.

"You tell me what you know, and I consider seventeen point five. But if I find out that you're lying to me, I'ma forget that you was a woman and treat you like the rest of the niggas in the street." Basco leaned back in his seat and looked out the window.

Chapter 6

Dave walked into the jewelry store on 8th and Market Street in Center City, Philadelphia. He was a regular customer there, so every retailer knew who he was. Every time he did a lick, he either put more ice in his chain or ended up buying something new, depending on how much money he got from the score.

He was sitting at the counter with Jim, one of the sales clerks, when through the front door came a breath of fresh air. She was gorgeous in every sense of the word, and whatever it was that made her smile the way she did, Dave envied it. She was accompanied by another woman and a gentleman, who had been the ones making her smile with whatever joke they just told. They walked right in behind her, laughing uncontrollably. Dave just hoped that the guy with her wasn't her boyfriend.

Her entourage spread out, but she walked right up to the counter where Dave was and glanced through the glass display at a pair of earrings. She looked so good that Dave was at a loss for words.

She caught him staring at her. She turned away with a weird look on her face, trying her best to avoid eye contact.

"Excuse me, Miss," Dave said, getting her attention before she walked away. "I swear to God, I'm sorry for staring at you, but I'm quite sure you already know the reason for it."

"And why is that?" she shot back, curious as to what else he had in his pickup line bag.

"You know that every day you wake up and look into that mirror, you say to yourself, 'Damn, I look good!' How can you blame anybody for staring at you when you look so beautiful?" he said in a sincere tone.

She smiled, accepting the compliment without judging whether he was speaking from the heart, or if it was just game. *He is kinda cute,* she thought to herself after she thanked him. "Is that ya normal pickup line when you meet a girl? Or do you have some more where that came from?" she asked, trying to make conversation.

"Look. My name is Dave," he said, extending his hand for a handshake.

"I'm Sarita," she returned, accepting his hand with a firm shake.

"I was wondering if maybe by some chance I could give you a call sometime, or maybe I can give you my number in case you felt like talking to someone when you get bored," he joked.

"How do you know that I'm not married, or even came here with my boyfriend? Don't you think you're pushing up on me a little hard?"

"I know that guy you came in with isn't your boyfriend, because he's over there kissing that girl. Second, any man would be a damn fool to let a woman like you walk around without a ring on her finger. It's either that, or he just don't know how good he has it. Either way, he's missing out on something good, because any man can see that you're wifey material."

"You got a little game," Sarita said with a smile, thinking about the last time anybody said something that sweet to her.

"Game! You think this is a game? Come here," he said, grabbing her pinky finger and pulling her closer to the glass. "You pick out any ring you want. I'm not asking you to marry me, but I just want to put something on ya finger for the meantime to keep niggas away from you until you at least get the chance to know me. If you find out in a few days that I'm not your type, you can keep the ring, no strings attached."

The things Dave was saying were blowing Rita's mind. No one had ever come on to her this strong before, and in an odd way, it felt kinda good. It made her want to play along with the Big-Willie talk just to see how far he was willing to go. It wasn't that she needed the ring, because she definitely could have bought every ring behind the glass if she wanted to. There was just something about him that made her feel girly-girly.

"That's cute," she said, pointing to a ring that cost $2,500.

Dave pulled out a wad of money from his back pocket and placed it on the counter. He told Jim to grab the ring, and when he did, Rita upped the stakes by pointing to yet another more expensive ring behind the glass that had a price tag of $5,500. She was just messing with him, but it didn't faze Dave one bit. He reached into his other back pocket and pulled out another wad of money and placed it on the counter, again telling Jim to grab that ring as well.

"Are you sure that's what you want?" he asked her, chuckling at Rita. "We can do this all day if you want."

This was getting too deep, but the deeper it got, the more Rita enjoyed the attention. It took Shay and Matt coming over to her to put out the sparks that were flying through the air between them.

"Re-Re, you found something that you like?" Shay asked, looking back and forth from Rita to Dave, then at the money on the counter.

It wasn't a game anymore. Rita was feeling Dave's swagger beyond her control. It wasn't the fact that he was willing to spend money on her, but it was more so the fact that she could see the sincerity in his actions about how badly he wanted a chance to get to know her. Any nigga that was willing to go that far was at least worth giving a shot.

"Yeah, girl, I think I found something," she said, staring into Dave's eyes and hardly worried about anything else around her.

"Well, c'mon, girl. We gotta go. You got people waiting on you," Shay said, trying to break the tension in the air.

Dave quickly pulled out his phone so that they could exchange numbers. He didn't even have to say a word. Rita had already started spitting out her number before he could say a word.

She started to walk away, but he stopped her. Not wanting to make a scene in front of everybody, he swiftly grabbed the most expensive ring off of the counter and placed it in her hand. She looked at him and smiled, then placed the ring into her pocketbook and walked out of the store.

Rita, Shay, and Matt pulled into the underground parking lot on 10th Street and parked on the second level, hoping to get the best position. Going into the jewelry store was just a front to waste time before meeting up with Basco to make the deal.

Matt got out of the car and went straight for the trunk, grabbed the 12-gauge pump from under the spare tire, and strapped a vest over his chest. Shay sat in the passenger seat with the door open, checking to make sure that she had a bullet in the chambers of her twin Glock 9 mm. She too put on a vest, tied up her Nike Air Max, and pulled her hair into a ponytail. Rita had a single Glock .40 with hollow tips in it. She declined to wear a vest because she'd rather look cute when she did the deal. All of these precautions were necessary when doing a drug transaction. One may never know when a deal can go bad.

Shay and Rita walked down to the first level, while Matt stayed back with the money. Rita designed every deal the same way just to make sure that the money wouldn't be exposed during the negotiation process. "If niggas get stupid, we take everything and walk," she told Shay, letting her know this could easily turn into a robbery.

When they got down to the first level, Basco beeped his horn, indicating which section of the parking lot he was in. Rita's high heels clicked throughout the parking lot as she approached Basco's Cadillac truck. He got out with two other men. All of them were strapped with automatic handguns. This was her third time dealing with Basco, and every time, it got more tense with all the guns out.

"What's good wit' you, Rita?" Basco asked, standing in front of the truck.

Basco was a short, fat, black-ass nigga with dreadlocks, and he always looked angry even when he was happy. He wasn't the biggest drug dealer in the city, but his supplier fed him large amounts of cocaine because he could get rid of it. Just about everybody in the city knew him, but not everybody messed with him, because the coke he had was so cut up that it was hard to make a good profit off of it by the time you got finished cutting it yourself. You really had to just give it away to make anything off of it. The first time he sold Rita anything, it was damn near pure. That's how most connects did it in the beginning just to get the clientele. But as soon as he served you a couple of times, he was up to his old tricks, and you were liable to get anything.

"Talk to me, Basco. What's the prices looking like today?" Rita asked, leaning up against a car parked next to the truck.

"That depends on what you're copping," he shot back.

"What are you going to charge me for fifty bricks?" she asked, catching his attention.

"You want fifty bricks?" he asked in shock. "I see you're steppin' up ya game a li'l, *mami*."

"Yeah, I want fifty, but it gotta be the same shit you gave me the first time. I wasn't impressed by the last shit I got from you."

"Nineteen K a brick," he shot out while looking off into the parking lot.

Rita was shocked at the number, seeing as how the number-one rule in the drug game was, when a larger purchase is involved, the more you cop, the cheaper it gets. The last time, Rita bought twenty-seven bricks, and the price was 19k. Plus, it wasn't all that good. These were the kinds of games that Basco was used to playing, and by the body language of his boys, it looked like he wanted to play an even more serious game, a game that might cost him his life if he didn't stop playing.

"Nineteen is too much. You gotta come down, or you can find somebody else to sell that bullshit to!" Rita said, leaning up off of the car.

"You got a nasty mouth for a female. When you're talking to a man, you need to learn how to humble yourself. Now, I'ma sit in the truck and discuss something wit' my boy. Maybe we can work something out."

Basco and his boys jumped into the truck. Shay stayed on point, keeping her eyes on them the entire time.

"Stay ready," Rita said. She looked over at Shay to see if she was up. This drug deal could easily turn into a robbery.

Before Shay could respond, Basco and his boys got back out of the truck. "I can go as low as eighteen point five if you got the money right now. Other than that, you can find someone else," Basco said, walking to the front of his truck.

"I'm not paying any more than seventeen point five," Rita demanded, puffing her chest out like she was ready for whatever.

Basco took that demand as an insult, and with his mind already made up from the conversation he had in the car with his boys, he was ready to turn it up on Rita.

Shay was the first person to notice Basco reaching in his pocket. The look he had in his eyes alerted her to what he was planning to do. Before Basco got the chance to get a shot off, Shay fired her gun, hitting him in the center of his chest. Rita quickly followed suit, pulling out her gun and focusing on the guy who was standing behind Basco, who also had his gun out.

Shay wasn't fast enough to react to the shooter on the passenger side of the truck. He squeezed off several rounds before she could turn to face him. The first bullet hit her in the chest, knocking her to the ground, while the other bullet hit her in the thigh while she was falling. She managed to get off two shots, striking him on the side of his head and in the hand that held his gun.

This was an all-out shootout at close range. At the same time Shay was falling to the ground, Rita was backpedaling with her gun blazing. She quickly jumped behind a car to get out of the line of fire coming in her direction. She could hear the bullets hitting the car she was hiding behind, and they were starting to get louder. She waited for the bullets to stop flying so that she could try to help Shay, who was lying on the ground a few cars back.

Silence finally took over the parking lot, and a thick cloud of gun smoke blanketed the air. The sound of the Cadillac truck starting up caught Rita's attention, but by the time she was able to get up from behind the car, the truck sped right past her. Shay got off a couple of shots, but they only hit the passenger door.

The driver of the truck knew for sure that he was about to get out of the parking lot in one piece, but as he came around the curve right before the ramp that led to the exit, Matt shattered his dream. Matt jumped from behind one of the parked cars and unleashed a series of shots from the 12-gauge shotgun. The buckshot ripped through the driver-side window and hit the driver everywhere from the neck up. His body went limp, and the truck crashed into a few parked cars before coming to a complete stop.

Rita got up from behind the car to see the guy that shot Shay was still alive. He was lying on the ground with blood leaking from the side of his head, and he was gasping for air. She didn't hesitate to walk over to him and put a bullet in the center of his head, this time finishing him off. She then walked over to Basco and did the same thing, just in case the shot to his chest didn't kill him.

"It went through!" Shay said, looking down at the blood coming from under her vest. "Damn, this shit burns!"

Rita ran to the truck and immediately popped open the trunk, not even fazed a little by the dead body slumped over the steering wheel. The two large duffel bags sitting on the floor looked like they contained more than fifty bricks of cocaine that she was trying to buy. She quickly opened up one of the bags, and it contained something much better than cocaine inside. It was money . . . a whole lot of it. She didn't even think to check the other bag after seeing that. She grabbed both of them and threw them over her shoulders, then rolled out.

***

Lump drove down the street in shock, seeing as how he had just witnessed Rita and her crew put down a vicious murder rap in the parking lot. He had been following Rita since she left the club last night, doing his homework as he usually did. Like a fly on the wall, he watched everything unfold, even the part when she grabbed the two duffel bags. It changed his whole outlook on her, but it sure didn't discourage him from sticking to his mission. If anything, it just made him sharper and more knowledgeable about how he planned to execute his plan. One thing for was sure. He was eager to see what was in those bags that Rita grabbed from the truck. Whatever it was, he wanted in on it before it got too late.

He jumped on the phone and immediately called Dave, hoping to change the day they would rob Rita to tomorrow, or possibly tonight, if push came to shove. If Lump had waited a few more seconds after Rita left the jewelry store, he would have seen Dave leaving after her.

Dave didn't answer the phone the first time, but Lump called right back, determined to talk to him. This time, Dave picked up.

"Yo, what's good, Cannon?" he answered, driving in his car on his way home.

"Man, I got to holla at you asap, my nigga. What are you doing tonight?"

"I'm busy tonight," he said, thinking about hooking up with Rita later on.

"Well, look. Tomorrow we need to have a sit down. Things just got real ugly wit' that situation I was telling you about."

"What you mean it just got ugly?"

"Trust me, it only got ugly for the better. Call me asap and I'll let you know what's poppin'. We can't do too much talking over the phone," Lump said, then hung up.

Lump sat at the red light, hoping that it would change before he lost Rita. He wanted to follow her every move at this point, and he definitely wanted to see where she was taking those bags.

He was so focused on keeping his eyes on Rita's car that he didn't even notice Isis walking up on the passenger side of his car. When she pulled the handle and the door flung open, it caught Lump by surprise. He couldn't reach for his gun fast enough, and by the time he got his hands on it, Isis was already sitting in the passenger seat with a chrome .45 pressed into his side.

"Drive," she said, seeing the light changing from red to green.

Obviously, Lump wasn't the only one following Rita this morning. Isis and Bones were pretty much on the same mission as Lump, but instead of going into the parking lot, they patiently waited outside. It didn't take long for Isis and Bones to realize Lump was following the same person they were.

"What are you doing following her for?" Isis asked, looking out of the back window to make sure Bones was still following behind them.

Lump just sat there and didn't say anything. He was more mad at himself that he had allowed Isis to catch him slippin' the way he did. This wasn't him. He was always careful about what he did, and for it to have been a girl sitting in his passenger seat with a gun pressed in his side made him want to reevaluate his tailing methods. That is, if he could manage to stay alive for this confrontation.

"I'm not going to ask you again. The next thing you're going to feel is a sharp pain running through your side, and the smell of gun smoke will fill your lungs."

"What does it look like I'm doing?" he replied with an attitude.

He didn't want to come out and say that he was following Rita, just in case Isis was a part of her entourage. He
didn't know, but Isis was thinking the same thing about
him, and before she revealed her cards, she wanted to get
some understanding about why he was there. Lump had
a feeling that Isis wouldn't shoot him while he was driving in downtown Philadelphia. There was a cop walking
the beat on damn near every corner, so the chances of her
getting away would be slim. It gave him a little time and
room to elicit some information of his own.

"Don't be a smart ass," she said, pressing the gun
deeper into his side.

"Hell, why are you following me, and who da fuck told
you to get in my car?" Lump asked, curious as to how the
predator became the prey.

"Shut up! I'm not following you. I'm following her," she
shot back, staring at the side of his face. "And if we're
following her for the same reasons, maybe we can work
something out."

"Something like what?" he asked, turning to briefly
look at Isis.

Isis was at the point where she could use a couple more
soldiers in her crew, especially somebody like Lump. She
could tell by the way he talked that he was about his work,
and the mere fact of the gun being pressed in his side
wasn't making him bend. With that, Isis knew Lump was
up to no good and having him on her team could be beneficial. At the same time, killing him on the spot wouldn't
make any difference to her either.

"Look, if you got plans on robbing her, I can help you,"
Isis said, easing the gun away from his side but keeping it
pointed in his direction.

"How can you help me when you just made me lose
her?" he said, not seeing Rita's car anywhere in sight.

"Don't worry. I know exactly where she's going. The only thing I need to know from you is if you're willing to be a part of my team."

If Isis had any idea who she was talking to, she probably wouldn't have asked Lump to be a part of her team. Lump had his own team, and what they were into was far more dangerous and made more money than what Isis had in mind. Lump was also smart, too, and he knew that the only way he was probably going to leave the car without a bullet in his side was if he complied and agreed to Isis's terms. Not only that, but if Isis was willing to help make the whole robbing process easier by providing good intel, he definitely was going to use her for what she was worth.

He had to admit, though, he thought Isis was cute despite the gun she had in her hand. The gangsta role she was playing was kind of a turn-on as well.

"I'm really feeling that scar," he joked, looking over at Isis while they sat at the red light. "Look, baby girl, I don't mean no disrespect when I tell you this, but I'm the boss of my own team. At the same time, if you wanna do some business wit' me, we can work something out. I think that when two great minds come together, it makes a hell of a brain," he said as he carefully reached over and grabbed his phone from the center console. "How about we exchange numbers? You give me a call later, and we can rap about it and work it out. In fact, I think me and you could make a good couple."

He smiled, fixing the rearview mirror so that both of them could see each other. Lump's demeanor was calm, cool, and collected the whole time, as though he wasn't being held at gunpoint.

Isis came with one objective but was about to leave under Lump's terms, which, by the way, wasn't bad. She found herself fighting the attraction she had to his handsome face, sexy voice, and his thug swag. It was crazy because when she looked in the mirror, they did look cute together.

Now wasn't the time to be thinking about a nigga, Isis thought to herself, pulling out her cell phone to get his number. It was either that or shoot him. It was like he took over the whole conversation. Seeing as how they were still downtown in the middle of the day with cops everywhere, Isis used her brain as well.

"When I call you, you better answer the phone," she said, getting out of the car and motioning for Bones to stop and pick her up.

Chapter 7

Shay lay on the table while Kimmy stitched up the bullet wound in her side. Kimmy was a friend of Rita's and was a registered nurse at Jefferson Hospital. This wasn't the first time that she had to sit in her living room and put somebody back together. The only difference today was that usually the bullet went in and out. The bullet that was lodged in Shay's leg was too deep to retrieve right now, so more than likely it would have to stay there for a while before she could get it removed.

"Girl, I'ma stop wearing my vest," Shay said jokingly to Rita, who had managed to dodge over ten bullets without having on a vest.

Rita still couldn't figure out why Basco would even think about trying to pull a stunt like that. All she wanted to do was cop fifty bricks of cocaine for a reasonable price and be on her merry way. Now, he and his boys were dead, and it was all over the six o'clock news.

"Where's Matt?" Shay asked while chewing on a few high-dose Motrin.

"He's counting the money," Rita answered with a big smile on her face.

"Money?"

"Yeah, baby girl. Some good came out of all this bullshit. The dumbest thing he could have done was to think that we was sweet. I think we may have hit the jackpot."

Matt walked into the room just as Kimmy was finishing up the last stitch. He looked tired, and his shirt was drenched with sweat. "There was $1.2 million in one bag, and thirty bricks in the other one. The coke isn't all that good, but it will sell," he said as he opened up a bottle of spring water to drink.

Everyone stared at each other for a moment, shocked at the amount of money he had just said was in the bag. Then, they all busted out laughing in celebration. Even Kimmy was laughing, thinking about how much she was going to get paid for her work.

During the celebration, Rita's cell phone started to ring. It was a number that she didn't recognize at first, but when she answered, she quickly remembered what Dave's voice sounded like. It was the kind of voice you couldn't forget. It was full of sweet, soulful bass.

"I'd like to speak with Sarita."

"I was wondering if you were going to call me today," she said while walking away from the group of people so that she could talk in private.

"I was wondering if it would be too much that we could meet up somewhere, while the night was still young."

"As much as I would like to, something came up this evening. I got to babysit my little sister," she said as she walked back over to Shay, who was now sitting up.

"I know how tough of a job that could be. Well, if you were to become free at some point, maybe you could give me a call back."

"If I was to get free later, I will definitely give you a call," Rita said, looking at Shay with a "schoolgirl crush" look on her face.

It had been two years since Rita had been in a relationship. After several dead-end relationships with some real ghetto bums, she swore off any and all relationships. She was happy to be a beautiful, free, single woman. She didn't need no man to define her. She knew she was a badass bitch. But there was something about Dave that turned on a switch in her heart to make her want to start dating again. Many men came on to her on a regular basis, but none of them were ever worth more than a phone conversation, and none of them definitely came with the right kind of game the way Dave did.

"Who was that?" Shay asked, squirming from the mild discomfort she felt when she sat up.

"That was Dave, the guy I met in the jewelry store earlier today. He wants to take me out, but I told him that I had to babysit you."

Shay looked at Rita and noticed a look in her eyes that she hadn't seen in a long time. She must have really liked this guy to have even mentioned his name, and to see her act in this manner made Shay want to encourage her sister to pursue the possibility of having a boyfriend. It had been too long, and Shay was getting tired of seeing her being alone.

"You should go out with him," she said, shocking the hell out of Rita with her approval. "After this near-death experience, you need to try and enjoy life."

"Girl, you know I don't go anywhere without you and Matt. I don't want to feel uncomfortable and ruin a good time."

Shay took a deep breath, then exhaled, shaking her head with a smile on her face. She got up off of the table and painfully walked into the living room and grabbed her gun from the table. Matt looked at her like she was crazy, thinking that she was willing to go out in the condition she was in. Shay walked back over to Rita and extended the gun for her to take it.

"This is just as good as me and Matt," she said, referring to the gun. "Go out and have a good time, big sis. We only live once."

Shay's words meant a lot to Rita, especially hearing her call her "big sis," something that she hadn't heard in years. Shay was right in so many ways when she talked about having fun and enjoying life. Rita had money, and she could have done just about anything she wanted to do, but what was the point of having money when you didn't have anybody to share it with?

Rita leaned in to kiss Shay on the forehead, and then stuffed the gun into her pocketbook with intentions on taking Dave up on his offer. "You just relax yourself and try to get some rest. You're a millionaire now!" she said with a smile as she walked toward the door and pulled out her cell phone to call Dave back.

Lump was thirsty. His mouth felt like the Sahara desert. He'd been riding around all night, trying to figure out where Rita had disappeared to. He lost her earlier that day after the parking lot shootout. He knew where she lived, but her car wasn't in the driveway like it normally was when she was home.

Lump couldn't wait to holla at Dave to let him know what went down, feeling that there was now more money involved than before. With that kind of knowledge, it would be impossible for Lump to sleep until that money became his.

He and Dave had been robbing shit since they were teenagers, and throughout the years, they only perfected their art and strengthened their loyalty to one another. The only thing that Lump didn't have much control over was his impatience. He sometimes was quick to jump the gun in certain situations, and he was very itchy with the trigger whenever gunplay was about to go down. The one thing Lump was good at with accurate precision was stalking. He would lay and wait on his prey like a cheetah hunting impala. And just like any wild animal, at the end of the day, he was going to kill his prey.

Rita's death was a sure thing after this robbery, and just because Shay was her best friend, if she got caught with her, she was getting killed as well. Hell, for a million, Matt was destined to taste dirt too!

Rita showed up at the place Dave invited her to just a bit after nine o'clock. She felt kind of funny, because this was her first date, and she didn't have time to go home and change her clothes or wash up. She was feeling a little un-fresh. She had on the same outfit she wore during the shootout, so there was definitely sweat seeping into her clothes.

The scenery was nice. It was a little restaurant in Center City that played soft music, and the lights were dim. Sort of romantic, but not too much for a first date. There were many couples having dinner together. The vibe was casual, which pleased Rita. She wasn't in no mood for some uppity restaurant with stuck-up waiters.

Dave was sitting in a booth with a window view, watching some of the drunk college kids walk by. When Rita walked through the door, he stood to greet her. She looked just as beautiful as she did earlier that day. He was turned on immediately.

Damn! Rita thought to herself when he stood up. He'd changed his clothes from earlier and looked even better. He smiled so brightly when she embraced him. The hug also gave her a little opportunity to feel parts of his body, which was tight, strong, and hard.

"Is it working?" Dave asked as he looked down at the ring he had bought her earlier.

"If you mean by keeping guys away from me, then I would have to say no. As long as a man sees a pretty face, a fat ass, and some big breasts, he could care less about what you got on ya finger. But I do think the ring is cute. That's why I have it on."

"Well, if you don't mind me asking, what is it that you do for a living? I can't seem to picture you working anywhere or for anybody," Dave asked, then gestured for the waiter to come over to their table.

"I'm a young, black entrepreneur. I run my own pharmaceutical company," she answered with a smile, thinking about how, in some odd way, what she was saying was actually kind of the truth. "And what about you, Mr. Dave? What is it that you do for a living?" she asked.

"I sell drugs, put guns in people's faces, and murder certain individuals for large amounts of money," he answered.

Rita's mouth dropped to the ground, and before she could respond to what Dave had just said, the waiter came over to the table to take their orders. She wasn't afraid of what he just said. In fact, she was kind of turned on by the whole bad-boy attitude. Her only concern was why would he tell her all of that, especially on a first date.

"Can I get you two something to drink?" the waiter asked, cutting short the silence at the table.

Rita thought about what Shay said about enjoying life and trying to have fun. It had been two years since Rita had a drink. But with the combination of celebrating the come-up from earlier and what Dave had just told her, she decided that one drink wouldn't hurt her.

"I'll have an apple martini," she said, and then dismissed the waiter before Dave could order anything. "Are you serious about what you said?" she asked, focusing her attention back on Dave with a curious look on her face.

"If I told you that I was serious, what would it change?" he asked with a serious face.

"First, I would like to know why you feel comfortable enough to tell me something like that. You've only known me for about eight hours, and we spoke for no more than ten minutes," she said.

"Well, if it was true, I probably would tell you the reason I told you was because I wanted to be truthful and honest with you from the beginning. I wouldn't want to start this relationship off by lying to you, so that later on down the line, you won't be able to say that you didn't know this about me. You would either accept me for who I am or reject me for what I am not—that is, if what I said in the beginning of this conversation was the truth."

Rita couldn't wait for her drink to get there. This conversation was getting real juicy, and the night was still young. His confidence had her feeling all types of ways.

The waiter came right on time, placing the large glass on the table. Rita chucked the straw and drank straight from the glass. She hadn't felt the butterflies in her stomach in a long time, and she hoped the alcohol would calm her down. Being ladylike was out the door.

"What if I told you that my 'pharmaceutical company' was a small drug empire, and me being an entrepreneur meant that I was the head of my empire?" she asked while twirling her finger around the rim of the apple martini glass. "Then, what if I told you that I killed two people, took sixty-five bricks and $1.2 million in cash from them, all about twenty minutes after I left you in the jewelry store this morning? What would you think?"

Dave cracked a smile, reached over, and grabbed the apple martini from her hand and took a gulp. He quickly thought about the cop cars racing up and down the street in Center City while he was on his way home. Then he thought about the breaking news on the TV right before he left the house to meet Rita. The news wasn't specific, but it did say something about a shooting downtown. "Well, if what you said was the truth, I would probably ask you to marry me," he said with a chuckle, but he was serious at the same time.

They both couldn't help but laugh at their hypothetical-but-true stories of what they did for a living. The connection between them was electrifying on the inside. But outwardly, they remained calm in speech. The level of connection they had throughout the night made it seem like they had known each other for years.

Rita looked Dave in his eyes. "Tell me, are you seeing someone?"

Dave shook his head. "It's been a minute since I've had someone special in my life. No one can understand what I'm going through with the lifestyle I lead. There ain't no days off. I'm tryin' to get in and out."

Rita smiled.

What you smiling for?" Dave asked.

"It's just that I feel the same way. Too many niggas think they all bad until they get with me. Then I find out they bums. They don't know what hard work is. They can't keep up with me. I'm about my business."

Now Dave was smiling.

The more they talked, the closer they became to one another. It is rare when two people connect on this type of level in such a short time, but when it does happen, it can produce some of the best relationships a man or woman could ever conjure. It's easy to fall for someone who understands you, and what goes on in your life, and someone who doesn't judge you or tries to manipulate your way of thinking just so that it seems like that person is better or smarter than you are. Two people who are on the same level in just about every aspect of life prove to be more suitable for one another, and Rita and Dave were just that, connecting on just about every aspect of life.

They went from having a late-night dinner to walking along the riverside in Penn's Landing. Rita never felt this comfortable with anyone, and without realizing it, she was letting her guard down, and it wasn't because of the two apple martinis she had during dinner.

Dave was also impressed with her and how she managed to maintain the kind of lifestyle she had while ripping and running around the streets. She was a keeper, and if he got the opportunity, he would do just that.

Cees hung up the payphone and got back in the car. "He's not answering the phone," he said. "He might be home asleep. It's still kinda early, and you know he don't do mornings."

"Yeah, but I spoke to him last night, and he knew we had a meeting," Lump responded and pulled out his cell phone in an attempt to try to call Dave himself. "This window of opportunity is going to close," he said with an attitude. "Dis nigga is starting to get lazy!"

Lump had finally caught up to Rita after doubling back to her house last night and finding that her car was in her driveway. During his time of surveillance, Shay and Matt pulled into the driveway at around three o'clock in the morning and entered the house. They remained there for the night. Lump wanted to get an early start on Rita this morning, but he had to get Dave and Cees and bring them back to Rita's house, so they would know what she, Shay, and Matt looked like. Having three targets made the robbery a little easier. Kidnapping one person could lead to the domino effect, making everybody else submit, especially if family was involved.

Lump had his plan already mapped out, and it was so simple. He and Cees could probably execute it themselves; it was that easy. All he had to do was stalk his prey until one of the sheep separated itself from the flock. It would be nice if Rita was that sheep, exposing herself and straying away from Shay and Matt, even if it were for a split moment. An abduction can happen at any time and any place, whether it's in a mall or at a gas station, in a supermarket or at a barbecue. Once you get caught slippin' and a gun is placed in ya face or in ya gut, most people are willing to comply, especially if the person holding the gun has no problem squeezing that trigger and killing you right where you stand if you act like you wanna draw a scene. For Lump, it really didn't matter who strayed away from the flock, just as long as it was one of them. If he had to, he'd pick 'em apart one at a time until he had everybody.

Dave cracked open his eyes and saw Rita lying next to him in the bed. She looked so beautiful while she was asleep. He never thought he would end up being in the position that he was in. And after last night, he truly understood that it was a privilege. He wondered what her reaction was going to be after waking up completely naked in her bed with a man she just met yesterday.

Rita's body was amazing, flawless in every sense of the word, and just to be sure that his eyes weren't deceiving him, he pulled back the sheet and exposed her body to the sunlight that peeked through the blinds. "Damn, you bad," he mumbled to himself and leaned over to kiss her on her shoulder blade.

"Good morning, handsome," she said with a smile on her face and moving over to get closer to his body. "What the hell were you looking for inside of me last night?" she joked, thinking about how deep Dave's dick was inside of her.

This wasn't what he was expecting from her when she woke up, but it definitely put a smile on his face knowing that she didn't have any regrets about what went down. The sex was incredible. Dave had touched places on Rita's body that had never been touched before, not even by her former boyfriend. He took his time and learned from the foreplay how her body ticked. It wasn't just a fuck. It was deeper than that, and by the condom still lying on the nightstand unopened, it proved that it was more personal than a one-night stand. Rita never felt this comfortable with a man to bring him to where she lived, let alone sleeping with him on the first night without using any protection. They lay there in bed, enjoying one another's company, hoping that nothing would prevent them from staying in that position for the rest of the day.

Someone pounding on the door dampened the mood. If Rita hadn't locked her door last night, Shay would have just busted into her room.

When Shay had returned home last night, she was so tired from the pain pills that she went straight to sleep. She'd heard Rita come home late, but she fell right back asleep. She was wiped out from the eventful day, and her body was so heavy from the surgery and medication.

Shay continued knocking on the door. "Re-Re!" Shay yelled. "C'mon, girl! Come to the door!"

"Give me a minute!" Rita yelled from her bed with an attitude. She was comfortable in bed with Dave. If she had her way, she'd stay there all day. There, in bed, she felt a million miles away from any stress.

"I take it that's your sister," Dave said, kissing Rita on the forehead.

"Yeah, and I know I'm about to hear an earful from her nosy ass!"

"Well, look. I'ma go in the bathroom and take a quick shower. I got a meeting today with my guys. I'm running late as it is."

"Let me find out you hit and run," she joked.

"Naw, not me! But I tell you what. After the meeting, I got somewhere special I want to take you. So if you can, try to clear ya schedule for the rest of the day."

"Yeah, I think I can make something happen. After I drop you off at your car, I'll take care of a few errands that I need to run. Then I'll be free."

Dave got up and shot right to the bathroom in nothing but his birthday suit. Rita couldn't help but laugh at how cute his butt was. She flashed back to the night before, when she was grabbing that butt while Dave was deep inside her. She quickly slipped on a robe, opened the door, and stepped out into the hallway to talk to Shay.

Shay could tell right off the bat that Rita had just gotten some dick. The smell emanating from the room and the flow in her eyes told the whole story without her saying a word. She tried to sneak a peek inside the room, just messing around, but Rita closed the door behind her with a funny-looking smile on her face.

"Who the hell you got in there?" Shay asked with a curious look, wanting nothing but the juicy details Rita was trying to hold back. "I know you ain't give dat man some pussy!" she blurted out in shock but laughing at the idea of Rita being a bad girl.

Rita quickly shushed Shay, hoping that she wasn't loud enough for Matt to hear her. Shay and Rita talked about everything ever since they were kids, but now wasn't the time nor the place to be having that conversation. Rita just wanted to enjoy the moment.

"We'll talk later." Rita was eager to join Dave in the shower, so she closed the door in Shay's face as she went back into her room. When she got to the bathroom, he was already lathered up with soap and looking sexy as hell through the glass shower doors. She slid the shower door open while disrobing herself seductively. She climbed in and immediately turned the second showerhead on.

This was the first time that Dave had a full view of Rita's body, and it was different. It was better, because there weren't any dim lights hiding certain parts of her body like there was last night. She looked so beautiful, and the water beading up on her body made it hard for him to resist, arousing his dick to becoming as stiff as a log. He couldn't help but to pull her closer to his body and press her chest up against his while he slowly swiped her bottom lip with his tongue.

He spun her around and bent her straight over as though he was about to hit her from behind, but he didn't. Instead, he squatted down behind her and stuffed his face inside her ass, licked the inside of her pussy as he spread her ass cheeks apart.

Rita held onto the shower knob for dear life as her body began to go through the motions. His tongue felt so warm inside of her, and the circular motions he was working began to send her body into convulsions. It felt so good that she reached back to grab his head, pressing his tongue deeper inside of her and making his chin rub against her clit.

"Oh! Oh! I'm about to cum!" she screamed as her legs began to lock and her toes started to curl. "Yes! Yes!" she yelled as her body exploded, sending cum all inside of Dave's mouth.

Her legs started to give out, but before she buckled to the shower floor, he was there to save her. He turned her around and lifted her in the air, slamming her back up against the wall. His dick was brick hard, and before she knew it, he stuffed it inside of her, thrusting and pushing his meat deep within her womb. She couldn't keep her tongue out of his mouth, and the more he long-stroked her, the more she moved, letting her honey drip all over his dick. He was giving her everything she'd been looking for, and at this point, she couldn't care less about who heard her screams.

Chapter 8

Lancaster was an untapped resource in the drug trafficking business, and it seemed like anybody that came out of Philadelphia to hustle there was successful. Lancaster was small, about fifty thousand people, half of which was Puerto Rican. The other half was black and white. Shay had been sliding out of Lancaster for the past few months, dibbing and dabbing with small amounts of drugs, during the time she was visiting her friend Rebecca. She went to school with Rebecca back in the day when Rebecca lived in Philly, but after she graduated high school, she moved out of Lancaster with her boyfriend. Rebecca was in the drug business but really didn't have the right kind of connect to flood her with the amount of drugs she was capable of moving.

Shay was supposed to meet Becca and her brother Rob at the Birds Nest bar to discuss the possibility of taking over the whole neighborhood by storm. Shay had plenty of coke and guns, and if necessary, a few goons from the city that was willing to put in work out of town for a couple of bucks.

Normally, Shay would travel out to Lancaster by herself, but tonight she had Matt with her, only because he wanted to be there in case she needed him. Ever since Rita gave Shay the okay to do her own thing on the side, Matt had been watching her every move, knowing that Shay had the potential to do something big on her own if she had the chance.

The bar was kinda packed when they got there. Rebecca was there waiting with her bother as planned. The introductions were brief, and they all sat at the round table stationed at the front of the bar where there wasn't a lot of people. A bottle of Grey Goose was ordered prior to Shay getting there. Rebecca poured everyone a shot. They all tapped glasses and took the shots.

"So, Becca, what's the prices looking like out here?" Shay grabbed the bottle of Grey Goose and poured herself another drink.

"Shay, it's nothing like the city. An ounce go for a grand, and when it's a drought, they go for thirteen hundred. The nickel bags from the hood go for twenty bucks out here, and the crackheads out here think that's a steal."

"So, who you hustle for?" Matt chimed in without remembering his manners.

"I don't hustle for nobody, baby boy. I'm just looking for a good sponsor I can rely on," Becca shot back, already irritated with Matt.

Rob began breaking down the logistics on Lancaster and the small block named Clay Street that had the potential to be turned into a gold mine. There wasn't a soul hustling on Clay Street, nor on the surrounding streets, so the need to have to take over an established strip wasn't necessary at all. This section of the neighborhood was pretty much open house to whoever wanted it. The problem was that nobody had the finances to do it.

"So, how much work do you think we need to get it started?" Shay asked. "The reason why I'm asking you is because I don't want to give you too little or give you too much."

"Well, you know me, Shay. I like to start from the ground up. You can give me seven grams, and I'ma make it do what it do." Becca downed a shot.

"Well, check dis out." Matt interrupted again. "I'ma bring a couple of my young bucks out here so they can run the block. All y'all got to—"

"Whoa, whoa, whoa. I can run my own block. Plus, we're not trying to draw that kind of heat out here," Rob spoke up, cutting Matt off.

"Shit, nigga, I don't know you," Matt said in an aggressive tone, seeing that Rob wasn't no kind of threat.

This meeting was starting to get out of hand, and it was all on account of one person. Shay looked at Matt in disgust, mad that he was embarrassing her the way he was. He was acting too aggressive for no reason, and in Shay's eyes, he really didn't have anything to do with what she had going on. He was in the way, and this was the reason why she never wanted to bring him out there with her in the first place.

"Look, everybody just cool out for a second," Shay said, trying to get some control of the situation. "Let's get something established right now, so it won't be no confusion about where we at with this. First and foremost, if we are going to be a crew, then we're going to need a boss. Every crew has a boss, and when it comes to this crew, I'm the boss. So that means nothing goes on without my approval, and when it comes down to this money we're about to make, it's going to get made the way I want it to be made. If everybody play the position they supposed to play, everything will be fine. But if anybody feel like they don't want to ride wit' me, then get up from this table and keep it moving."

Everybody got quiet at the table, but nobody moved. Matt was clearly upset with the way Shay was talking, but he kept his ass sitting at that table. If anybody knew better than to doubt her skills of getting money, it was Matt. He knew firsthand what Shay was capable of doing.

Becca also knew a thing or two about Shay, and it wasn't just about how she could make money. Becca knew how street-smart Shay was and her ability to make good decisions in tough situations. Becca knew one thing for sure, and that was if it came down to it, she could trust Shay with her life. That's the reason why she stayed. Rob just stayed because Becca did.

"Now that we got that established, here's how it's going to be," Shay said, looking around the table before pouring everybody another shot of Grey Goose.

Rita took Dave out for a late dinner that evening. They went to Dwight's, a BBQ rib spot in West Philly. It was nice outside, so the decision to eat on the hood of the car was Dave's. The sounds of smacking and sucking on the tasteful BBQ sauce filled the air, and the only words being said from either of them was, "Dis shit is good." Rita wasn't shy when it came to eating in front of anybody, and it brought a smile to Dave's face seeing her dig in the way she was.

"Oh, shit," Rita said in a low voice, seeing the familiar cop car creeping up Lancaster Ave, headed directly toward her car.

"What's wrong?" Dave asked, looking around in a somewhat paranoid state.

The unmarked car stopped right in front of Rita's car, and getting out of the driver's side was Mozar. Rita tossed the rib back into the box, instantly losing her appetite. The day had been going good up until now, and Dave still wasn't aware of what was going on.

"Dwight's! I love Dwight's," Mozar said as he approached Rita's car. "And you, you must be the infamous boyfriend everybody's talking about," Mozar taunted, leaning up against the car.

Rita was tired of Mozar, and she really didn't know what she did to him to make him hate her so much. She wasn't as big of a drug dealer as Mozar was making her out to be, and besides that, there were plenty of other drug dealers in the neighborhood that he could have harassed instead of her. Mozar acted as if the beef he had was personal. It only confused Rita, because he never really asked for anything specific or made any indications as to why he was focusing on her so much.

"You know, this is starting to get a little ridiculous," Rita said, annoyed with Mozar and his frequent pop-up games.

Mozar took a good look at Dave then walked around to the passenger side of the car. His partner stayed on the driver side with Rita. He pointed to the hood of the car for Dave to put his hands on it for a pat search. Dave looked at him like he was crazy and continued to eat his ribs like he didn't hear a word he was saying.

"Don't play the tough guy role. Just put ya hands on top of the car," Mozar said, attempting to grab Dave's arm.

Dave thought about the gun he had in the car and the possibility of Rita having her gun as well. The best thing for him to do was comply in hopes that they would search him and keep it moving. Dave didn't have the slightest idea that Mozar and Rita had somewhat of a history, and from his eyes, Mozar was just another dick-head cop trying to make trouble.

He placed his hands on the car and allowed Mozar to frisk him, all the while still sucking the BBQ sauce off the rib. Mozar looked up at his partner, who was busy having Rita empty out her pockets.

"I'm only cuffing you for safety reasons. You are not under arrest."

Dave knew it was some bullshit behind it. Mozar's partner also put the cuffs on Rita, telling her the same thing.

"We didn't do anything to be placed in handcuffs. And we damn sure didn't do anything for you to be searching my car," Rita told Mozar, who was looking around inside of the car.

"Ohhhhh, somebody's packing." Mozar pulled a Glock 9 mm from the center console. He had a big smile on his face. "Seek and ye shall find." He dangled the gun in the air so that everybody could see it.

"You know, that's funny, because I didn't see you get a warrant to search my car," Rita taunted back, reminding Mozar that she knew a little bit about the law.

"Well, you should have learned that anything that's in plain view is fair game in a warrantless search. Ain't that right, partner?" he yelled out to his partner.

"That's right. That gun was in plain view when I looked in the car. I guess the only other thing that needs to be determined is, who's going down for it?"

Although the gun was being illegally possessed, Mozar and his partner were playing a little dirty. The gun was never in plain sight. Mozar had to open up the center console to see what was inside of it. It may not seem like an important fact right then and there, but in the court's eyes, it would make a hell of a difference in determining whether the search was lawful.

Dave looked at Rita, and she looked back at him. The gun in the center console was Rita's. Dave's gun was still tucked away under the passenger-side seat. It wasn't a need for both of them to go to jail for one gun. Somebody had to step up and take the beef.

The ride back to Philly was quiet for Shay and Matt. Matt was feeling some type of way about how Shay had bossed up on him in front of the out-of-towners. He felt disrespected and belittled, especially having all this lip coming from a female.

"Don't take this personal, but I don't think you should worry about what I got going on out here," Shay said, breaking the silence in the car. "I know that you're my man, and I know that you might be worried about my safety, but just let me deal with Lancaster by myself."

"Let you deal with Lancaster by yourself," Matt repeated sarcastically.

Lancaster was probably the only chance Matt was going to have if he wanted to come from under Shay and Rita's shadow. This was his chance to become a boss in his own right, and seeing as how his girl was the one who could give him the opportunity to do so, he thought that it was grimy. He didn't even understand or care that Shay was trying to find her own way.

Shay wanted to finally come from under Rita's shadow and be her own boss. Respectfully, she waited her turn, and now was her time. Not even Matt was going to be able to stand in her way.

"You're no different from the rest of da bitches I used to fuck wit'. After a while, y'all all think that you're better than a nigga," he said, looking off down the highway.

"That's not fair, Matt. I stood by your side when you didn't have a dime."

"Maybe I was on the wrong side all this time," he said, cutting her off. "Isis was right about y'all bitches."

He couldn't get another word out before the first smack landed on the side of his face. It really didn't faze him until a number of smacks, followed by punches, started flying his way. The car swerved as Matt tried to slip the punches, hoping that he could stop the car before Shay made them crash. He threw a punch back at her, striking her right on the jaw. It didn't stop her from swinging, but it definitely slowed the punches.

"Fuck you, Matt! Fuck you, Matt," she yelled, throwing her last punch before Matt could get the car to come to a complete stop.

He quickly threw the car in park and wasted no time grabbing her by the neck. "You crazy bitch. You could have just killed both of us," he yelled, choking her with both hands.

He took his hands from around her neck and mugged her head. Her tears meant nothing to him.

Tonight might have been the straw that broke the camel's back. To even mention Isis's name in the same breath as Shay's was more than an insult, more than disrespect. It was almost as though he was picking a side to be on. At least that's the way Shay was taking it. Either way, tonight Matt said something that he couldn't take back, and there was nothing he could say, nothing he could do, that would make Shay forgive him. He signed his walking papers.

Once a cop steps out of his uniform and attempts to roll with the wolves, their lives and wealth are fair game. Their conduct determines whether or not they're acting in accordance with the judicial system or on their own accord. Mozar definitely wasn't acting in accordance with the law, and for that, he subjected himself to the streets. The badge he wore was pointless from here on out.

Dave left the Roundhouse police station around 2:00 in the morning. He stepped up and took the gun case for Rita, even though it belonged to her. With the kind of money and lawyers he was used to dealing with, the case probably wouldn't make it to trial. It was merely an inconvenience to have to sit in a dirty holding cell. Bail definitely wasn't an issue either, knowing that Rita would be waiting at the courthouse with however much it was going to cost.

Mozar had it out for Rita, and during the whole ride to the police station, Mozar bragged to Dave about how Rita didn't have that much longer on the streets. His partner almost slipped up and gave the reason why they were on Rita's back so hard. Whatever he was about to say most likely didn't have anything to do with an investigation, because of the way Mozar gave him a look to say, "Shut da fuck up."

"What the hell was that all about?" Dave asked Rita as he walked out of the police station.

"I don't know, Dave, but this cop got it out for me," she said. She was having just as much trouble as Dave making sense of everything.

As they walked toward the car, the same Crown Victoria pulled right up beside them, damn near hitting them. To no surprise, it was Mozar and Seal. He only rolled his window down instead of getting out.

"When you're ready to play by my rules, we can all get along," he said, not even looking at Rita. "I'll be in contact."

Mozar rolled his window up and pulled off, leaving Rita and Dave in the parking lot, looking even more confused. Whatever it was that he wanted, he'd been barking up the wrong tree. He wasn't only irritating Rita right now, but he was also working on Dave's last nerve. Mozar didn't have the slightest idea about who Dave was and how ugly it could get in a New York minute fucking around with him.

Chapter 9

Rita pulled up to her grandmother's house for an afternoon lunch. They've been having these lunches every Saturday for the past few months. It brought them closer together, and during these times, Rita got a chance to learn about her roots. Grandma Scott talked about everything Big Wink used to do when he was a baby. This was also the time that Big Wink would call and talk to Rita, seeing as how he didn't want to draw any attention from the Feds on Rita by calling her personal phone.

When Rita got out of the car, the first thing she could smell coming from the house was fried chicken breast, eggs, and home fries. There was a car in the driveway, but she didn't know who it belonged to. She thought that it may have been one of her many uncles who usually showed up whenever Grandma was in the kitchen, but as soon as Rita walked through the door, the first person that she saw was Isis, sitting at the dining room table. Grandma was sitting there too, and they were going through a photo album, looking at pictures of Isis's dad, Marvin, who died of cancer a few years back.

"My grandbaby," Ms. Scott announced when she saw Rita. "We was waiting for you to get here. I wasn't going to start serving the food without you."

Rita couldn't take her eyes off of Isis, even while giving her grandmother hugs and kisses. Isis stared back at Rita with a devious grin on her face, knowing she was well protected by the security of their grandmother. She knew Rita wouldn't try anything crazy in front of her.

"Hey, big cousin," Isis said with a smile on her face like she was happy to see her. She did it only to taunt Rita, hoping she could make her fly off the handle in front of Grandma.

Rita didn't even speak back, not wanting to waste her breath. She made her way over to the table where the family pictures were out, still not taking her eyes off of Isis. She was burning up inside, and all she could think about was the time Isis tried to shoot and kill her.

It wasn't a secret. Isis tried to kill Rita, and now she had the nerve to show up at a place she knew Rita would be. Rita had no idea that Isis wasn't the cause of this meeting, but rather their grandmother set today up because she wanted to see both of her only living grandchildren. Isis merely accepted the invitation.

Rita looked down at the pictures sitting on the table, and a picture of her dad sitting with Isis's dad was smack dab in the middle.

Rita's grandma saw her looking at the pictures. "Those two boys would play trains all the time. I'd have to pry them away from playing when it was time for dinner. They refused to stop with their trains. It was so cute. I'd peek in on them, and they'd be so engrossed in their story."

Her stories were enlightening, but not enough for Rita to feel any sympathy toward Isis about what she was going to do to her.

"I talked to uncle Wink," Isis said, getting Rita's attention immediately. "He said he was calling back in a hour, and that was about thirty minutes ago."

"Well, I'ma finish putting the food together so I can feed y'all," Ms. Scott said, getting up to go in the kitchen.

"Do you need me to help?" Isis offered, but she was quickly flagged off by her grandmother.

When she turned around from watching her grandma go into the kitchen, she saw that Rita had one of her hands under the table. Rita had pulled the .40-cal from her pocketbook and had it pointed right at Isis under the table. It didn't bother Isis one bit. She even looked under the table to see the gun pointed directly at her, then picked her head up with a smile on her face.

"So, you gonna shoot me, or keep faking under the table like I'm supposed to be scared?"

The sound of the safety being taken off the gun made Isis realize that Rita wasn't doing any faking. She was two seconds away from emptying the whole clip inside of Isis. The only thing that snapped Rita out of her trance was Grandma Scott bringing a pitcher of Kool-Aid into the room.

"I'll be back in about five minutes with y'all's food," she said, heading back into the kitchen.

"Thank you, Grandma," they both said simultaneously.

By the time she focused her attention back on Isis, the cocking of a gun sounded off under the table. Rita slipped and gave Isis enough time to pull the chrome .45 from out of her front pocket, pointing it directly at her under the table.

"I'm not faking. If you want to get it poppin' up in here, all you got to do is pull the trigger. We both be some dead bitches up in here," Isis declared, serious about what she was saying.

It became quiet at the table. Rita was really considering taking Isis up on her offer. The phone ringing on the table broke the silence in the room, and Grandma Scott yelled from out of the kitchen, telling somebody to answer the phone. Isis was the first to volunteer to answer the phone, still keeping her gun pointed at Rita under the table.

"Hello," she answered. "Oh, hey, Uncle Wink. Yeah, she's right here," she said, passing Rita the phone.

Rita grabbed the phone, still keeping her gun pointed at Isis. "Hey, Daddy," she said, staring Isis in her eyes.

"How's my princess?" Big Wink asked, happy to hear his daughter's voice.

"I'm good. Did you get the money I sent you yesterday?"

"Yeah, I got it, but I thought I told you not to send me money. Trust me, baby girl, ya dad is doing fine."

"Well, whether you like it or not, I'ma hold you down. I talked to ya lawyer last week, and he told me that your appeal looks good. I gave him some money too."

"Thanks, princess, but you have to stop giving him money, and I'm damn sure goin' to tell him to stop taking ya money, because he's been paid for my case. All I'm doing is waiting to hear something back from the appeals court."

"I know, Dad. I just want you to come home. I miss you," Rita said, her eyes starting to tear up.

Rita did miss her dad. He'd been gone for a few years now, and it wasn't a day that went by that she didn't wish he was there to help her through life, especially during times like the one she was having with Isis. Visits and phone calls meant a lot, but his physical presence was much needed.

Rita sat there and talked to her dad the whole fifteen minutes with her gun still pointed at Isis. She still wasn't sure whether or not to shoot her now and get it over with. Knowing that Isis had a gun pointed at her kinda changed things. She only wanted to do the shooting and not get shot in the process.

As soon as Rita got off the phone with her dad, Grandma Scott came into the room with the food. Understanding and only sympathizing with the fact that this was her grandmother's house, Rita decided that this wasn't the right time or place to kill Isis, even though she wanted to so bad. She had too much respect for Grandma Scott and her dad to have a shootout right there.

"Out of respect for my grandmother, we're going to finish this shit as soon as we leave here," Rita said, putting the safety back on her gun and placing it into her pocketbook.

"I agree. We can meet right down the street at the park and do what we gotta do," Isis confirmed, putting her gun back into her pocket.

They both sat there and enjoyed lunch with Grandma Scott like nothing was wrong. They even managed to put on a good show, smiling and laughing together at Grandma Scott's jokes. But in the back of both of their minds, they were conjuring up a strategy to kill one another in the park in a couple of hours.

Cees stayed a good distance behind Ashley as he followed her down the highway. Nothing was the same in their household, and for the most part, it looked like the relationship was pretty much over. It wasn't because Ashley didn't want to stay together, because she did. She wanted to work things out and go back to the way things used to be, but Cees just couldn't let it go. It was hard for him to deal with the fact that he had no idea who she was messing around with, and even though he probably wanted to kill him, it shouldn't have made a difference to Ashley what happened to him.

Ashley went out again this afternoon and left the house with the same vibe she had when she was cheating.

"Where you going?" he asked.

"Oh, umm, I got some stuff to do."

"Like what? I can come with you and help." He was testing her.

Ashley started hurrying around the house like she was looking for something. Cees didn't buy the act for a second.

"Oh, that's OK, baby. I can take care of it. It's boring girl stuff. You wouldn't have fun."

"You looking for something?"

"No. I'm making sure I have everything I need." She looked at herself one last time in the mirror. "Don't know how long I'll be out. Take care of the baby and have fun. Don't wait for me." She walked out of the house.

By leaving the baby behind, she thought that it would keep Cees in the house while she was gone, but that wasn't a good way of thinking. Cees was on her heels. With the baby in the back seat and a gun on his lap, he raced down the highway in hopes that she was going to lead him straight to the nigga she'd been seeing. His mind wasn't made up completely about whether or not he was going to kill whoever she was cheating with, but he definitely wanted to catch her in the act.

"You see, son, when you get older and you find a nice girl and love her with all of your heart, you'll understand why I'm doing what I'm doing," Cees told his baby son, who was sitting in his car seat, playing with his pacifier. "I love ya mom, and I give you my word that I won't kill her, but I can't say the same thing about the nigga she's been creeping wit'."

Cees was talking to his son like he was old enough to understand what was going on. He really was just trippin' out, because he didn't have anybody else to talk to. He watched as Ashley got off on the Germantown exit and made her way up Wayne Avenue. He didn't know too many people that lived up that way, and the only time he really came to Germantown was when he was with Lump. Lump had a house in every part of the city, including Germantown. Cees was kind of familiar with the area, seeing as how this was the house they normally meet up at after doing a job.

He called Ashley's phone to see if she would tell the truth about where she was, as he followed behind her at an unnoticeable distance. It took a few rings, but she finally picked up the phone, seeing that it was Cees.

"Hey, babe," she answered, driving down the street, unaware Cees was right behind her.

"Yo, where are you? I was going to ask you before you left the house if you, me, and the baby could go out today," Cees said, keeping his eyes on her car.

"I'm pulling up in front of Keisha's house right now. We were supposed to be going to lunch and possibly get our nails done today. Can we do it tomorrow?" she asked like her plans for today were far more important than spending time with her family.

Cees looked on into the busy traffic, thinking to himself how much of a liar Ashley had become. Keisha lived in North Philly, not Germantown, and it wasn't but two days ago she just got her nails done. To Cees, it only meant that he was closer to finding out what he wanted to know.

Chapter 10

Rita looked down at her phone to see that Dave was calling. She had just left the park where Isis stood her up. When Grandma Scott had asked Rita to come in the kitchen and help her with the dishes, Isis took the opportunity to disappear out of the house before Rita got back into the room. She wasn't surprised. She knew Isis was a scared bitch.

"Hey, stranger. You haven't called me all day. I was wondering what happened to you," Rita said, leaving the park and getting back into her car.

"Yeah, I got a little caught up. But I was wondering if we could meet up. I wanted to take you somewhere," he said, hoping she would agree.

Rita was really starting to have a good time with Dave. He was a cool dude, and it had been a while since she had this much fun with anybody. She'd just met him a couple of days ago, and they were already planning their second date. It was kind of what Rita needed to balance out her life. She needed somebody to be there for her for a change, instead of always being there for everybody else. With Dave, she didn't have to spend her money or take control like she had to do in other relationships. All she had to do was show up and Dave was taking care of the rest.

"Just give me a time and a place and I'll be there," Rita said with a big smile on her face.

Talking to him made her forget all about the streets and the problems she had going on, including the one she had with Isis. She really didn't feel like chasing Isis around, and it kind of made Rita regret not shooting her in the house when she had the chance. It was a sure thing that if the opportunity ever presented itself again, she wouldn't hesitate pulling the trigger, no matter where she was at.

Isis took that brick she got from Basco and did wonders with it in Southwest Philly. Seeing as how he was dead now, she didn't have to worry about paying him back. Her block was doing good numbers, and she was even starting to expand to a couple more blocks in Southwest. Not only that, but her crew was getting larger. A lot of people started to cling to her, and the love she was giving out showed with loyalty. She was still far from having the kind of money Rita had, but she was starting to become comfortable in her own skin.

But even with her comfort level established, the situation between her and Rita was far from over with. It wasn't going to stop until somebody got killed, and with every day that went by, Isis was getting her money up as well as her army so that she could go head up with Rita with an even chance of winning.

Isis lay in the bed, watching *CSI Miami,* when her doorbell rang. She got up to answer the door, and when she opened it, Matt was standing there. She wasn't expecting him to come over, but she allowed him in anyway. There were things she wanted to discuss with him about what happened with the whole Basco situation. Matt, of course, was there for other reasons, and Isis was well aware of it. She really didn't mind, just as long as she got what she wanted out of the deal, which was information.

Honestly, Isis wasn't even feeling him like that anymore. She realized the importance of loyalty and could see how Matt lacked that for his girl, Shay. She still found him attractive, but that was about it.

"Yo, before we get into all of that, I need to talk to you about something," Isis said, pushing Matt off of her as she lay on the bed. "I need to know what happened with Rita and Basco."

"Well, if I tell you, I got to kill you," he joked, removing his shirt in the process. "I can tell you that it was a lot of money involved."

"A lot of money like how much?" she asked with a curious look on her face.

"If I tell you, what are you going to do for me?" Matt said in a seductive way, trying to take off Isis's t-shirt.

The way he talked reminded Isis of Basco and how desperate he was for a shot of her good-good. She knew she had Matt right where she wanted him, and with his dick rock hard the way it was, she could get him to tell her any and everything she wanted to know. He did just that.

"We went there to score some product. Things went sideways real quick. You know how that go. Next thing I know, we robbing him."

Isis shook her head in disbelief.

"That's what I'm sayin'. It didn't need to be like that. But once we counted up the money, I damn sure forgot about that. We scored one point two mill and a bunch of coke. I'm sittin' on a nice stack now."

"Sounds nice. Tell me what she sayin' about me."

"She hate you. She always talking about killing you. But, not just killing, torturing."

"How does she plan to do it?"

"She hasn't said yet. All I know is she's obsessed with it. Now, let me get some of that ass." He smiled.

"Hold on. Don't you and Shay get down?"

"You know she ain't nothin'. I haven't loved her in a minute. I'm stickin' around because it's good for my pockets. She ain't got nothin' on you, though." He wrapped his arms around Isis's waist.

He pretty much told everything, all to feel his dick inside of Isis. He didn't even know that the more he talked, the more Isis was disgusted with him. Loyalty was one of the things that attracted her to him, and now his disloyalty was pushing Isis away, even if it was benefitting her.

Hearing that, Isis reached over and grabbed her phone off the nightstand. $1.2 million was a lot of money, and if Matt was telling the truth, she knew exactly who to call. She couldn't dial Lump's number fast enough.

Matt didn't even care that she was on the phone. He just continued to kiss all over Isis's breast and neck, paying no attention to who she was calling.

"Yo, what's good," Lump said, answering the phone like he had a lung full of weed smoke.

"I got some business to discuss wit' you. When do you think we can meet?" Isis said, sounding irritated because Matt was trying to kiss her lips.

"How important is it? Because I'm a little bit busy right now," he said, looking out of his window to see a certain car pull up.

"$1.2 million dollars important," she said, pushing Matt's head down toward her pussy for some head.

Matt still wasn't paying attention to what Isis was saying. His face was buried in her pussy as she continued to talk to Lump on the phone. Lump, on the other hand, was paying good attention to what she said, especially the part about $1.2 million. For that kind of money, there was no need to sit around and wait for his company to come over.

"Meet me at The Bottom of the Sea on Fifty-second Street in thirty minutes. It's a small crab shack."

"I know exactly where that is," she said, cutting him off. "I'll see you there," Isis told Lump before hanging up the phone.

She looked down at Matt, who was still eating her pussy, and it wasn't until that moment she started to feel the tingling sensation of an orgasm coming on. She grabbed the back of his head with both of her hands as though she was fucking his face. The one thing Matt was good at and could do very well was eat pussy, and before she ruined his day by getting up to leave without letting him fuck, she was going to enjoy busting a nut in his mouth. Fucking was going to have to wait for another time; that is, if there was going to ever be one.

Cees watched as Ashley pulled over on Wayne Avenue near Walnut Lane. It was only a couple of blocks away from where Lump had a house. Cees pulled over too, thinking to himself that this was it. His heart was racing, and his hands started to sweat on the steering wheel. He looked back at his son, who was looking back at him, laughing at the sight of his daddy.

"Stop laughing at me, boy," he said, making a funny face at his son. "I know I'm crazy. I know I'm crazy." He smiled with love at his boy.

He turned around in his seat to focus back on Ashley, who hadn't left her car yet, nor did anybody come to it. She sat there for about five minutes, and then pulled off again. Cees pulled off right behind her. Two minutes went by before Cees' phone started to ring. He grabbed it and saw that it was Lump, probably wanting to give an update on the situation with the upcoming lick.

"What up, my nig," Cees answered, keeping his eyes on Ashley's car going back down Wayne Ave.

"Yo, I need you to meet up wit' me asap. I got a lot of good news about that situation, and I believe it's time we take care of that demonstration," he told Cees as he was getting dressed.

"Yeah?"

"Yeah! And I think this is the one that could put us in retirement, ya dig. I want you to meet me on Fifty-second Street at the crab spot in about thirty minutes. I'll give you all the details then. And see if you can reach Dave. I've been trying to call this nigga since yesterday."

"All right, I got you. I see you in a half," Cees said then hung up.

Cees looked up and found himself following Ashley back onto the highway, heading back home. He wondered if she had seen him and decided to cut her plans short, or if he'd missed something that already happened. It bugged him because he knew she didn't come all the way out there for nothing.

Right then, his phone started ringing again. It was Ashley. He quickly answered it, almost ready to blow his cover and ask her why she was in Germantown, but he stayed cool.

"Hey, babe," he answered, looking in his rearview at his son.

"Well, I was calling to let you know that Keisha decided not to go anywhere, so I was wondering if you still wanted to go out."

Cees took the phone away from his ear, wondering what the hell was going on. Was she really going to meet Keisha or not? Why was she all the way over in Germantown? Cees was confused. Something wasn't right, but he failed to prove anything right then. Nothing happened. He was going to have to wait to catch her doing something. He was starting to look at her in a whole new light. No matter what happened, he knew this relationship was over.

"Naw, I can't do it. I made other plans," he said with an attitude, knowing he was about to meet up with Lump. "I got the baby. I'll call you when I'm on my way home."

"Wait, don't—Hello? Hello?" Ashley yelled into the phone, mad that Cees hung up in her ear.

She tried to call him back, but his phone went straight to voicemail. She felt bad, thinking she had messed up again. It seemed like everything she was doing only made things worse, even when she thought she was doing the right thing.

Chapter 11

Mozar jumped out of the shower and headed to his bedroom to get dressed. Like a typical family man, he engaged in the morning routine of helping his wife get the kids ready for school, prepared breakfast, and took the trash out. The sound of his phone vibrating on his nightstand caught his attention. It wasn't the standard-issue phone from the force that was ringing. It was his personal phone.

He looked down at his phone, curious as to the unfamiliar 215 number that popped up on his screen.

"Mozar!" he answered, standing in nothing but his towel wrapped around him.

"Detective, it's so good to hear from you this morning," Rita calmly said into the phone. "In case you don't know who this is, it's Rita, the one you so badly have a crush on."

That was a shocker to Mozar. She would be the last person he thought would call him on his personal phone, but he was also curious to find out the reason for the call.

"Oh, don't worry about how I got ya number. You're not the only one capable of gathering information."

"What do you want?" he asked.

"Well, you know my boyfriend got a hearing this morning, and I think that it would be to your benefit that you didn't show up."

"What makes you think that it would benefit me? And please, don't sell me no death threats. I get those too often."

Mozar was about to see exactly what it felt like to be amongst the street runners. It was true that he had somewhat of the upper hand because of his badge, but his disadvantages lay in his lack of ability in having the killer instinct. It was not just the courage to kill someone who pulls a gun out on you, and you shoot him because of fear, like most cops do. But it was the ability to kill anybody at any given time for no godddamn reason at all. That was what separated the thugs from the civilians.

"Your son's school bus should be pulling up in front of your house any minute now. It would be tragic if a stray bullet hit him in the top of his head," Rita threatened, but she was actually ready to go the extra mile.

Mozar walked over and grabbed his gun off the night-stand, went over and looked out of his bedroom window. He couldn't see anybody as he looked up and down the street.

"Honey, breakfast is ready," his wife yelled up to him.

Mozar didn't hear her. He was too focused on his phone call.

"You know you're playing a dangerous game fucking with me, little girl."

"Yeah, yeah, yeah. Listen up! You're a crooked cop, and I know how to deal with crooked cops. I'ma give you one chance and one chance only for us to do business together. After that, all bets are off and whatever happens, happens."

"Business with you?" he asked with a chuckle. "Little girl, you can't afford me," Mozar shot back, still looking out the window for any movement.

"Yeah, well, meet me at Christy Rec Center in an hour and let's see how much my money talks. Consider the five K you took from my sister as a down payment for you not showing up for court today," she said and hung up the phone.

Rita wanted to get to the bottom of why Mozar was on her top the way he was. The way he was going so hard and so dirty, there had to be somebody else behind it. Mozar hadn't asked for a dime of Rita's money yet, but at the same time, she never offered any. One thing was a guarantee at this point, and it was that Rita got his undivided attention.

Chapter 12

Bones walked out of the Chinese store on Greenway Avenue, one of the blocks Isis owned in Southwest Philly. Traffic was moving fast, and it seemed like a never-ending flow of crackheads walking up and down the street. He watched as one of his workers served fiend after fiend, and it made him feel good about the direction his block was headed, thanks to Isis.

"One-time! One-time!" a lookout yelled, seeing a cop car creeping down the street.

The 12th district cops were the worst cops in the city, next to the 35th district. They did more dirt than the criminals did on the streets, and the saddest part about it was they got away with it. Usually, the corner didn't stop moving if it was a single, regular cop car, but being as though it was two coming down the block and a third one sitting at the top of the block, it kinda caught everyone's attention.

The first thing that came to Bones' mind was that it was a raid. All he could think about was the gun he had on his hip and the history behind it. If they even thought about getting out of their cars for any type of reason, a foot chase was mandatory in Bones' eyes.

The first cop car went by, and the officers inside just did a lot of staring as if they were looking for somebody specific. It was the second cop car that made the difference. It pulled right up in front of Bones and stopped. Before the passenger-side cop got his hand on the door handle to open it, Bones took off running, dropping his iced tea and cigarettes in the process. He didn't waste time or think twice about it. He took off so fast and covered so much distance within the first few steps, the cop didn't even want to get out of his car to chase him. He blew right past the first cop car that went down the block, then turned onto 56th Street.

"Suspect running eastbound on Fifty-sixth Sreet," the cop yelled out over his radio. "He's wearing blue jeans, white t-shirt, and white sneakers."

One cop actually jumped out of his car and began chasing Bones on foot. It took a while, but the weed, alcohol, and lack of fitness caught up with him. He knew that he would only get one chance to get rid of the gun, so as he turned into the alleyway, he tried to throw the gun on the roof. The gun made it on the roof but slid back off of it because the roof was slanted. The gun almost hit the cop that was chasing him in the head, and when it hit the ground, the gun actually went off.

"Shots fired! Shots fired!" another cop yelled over the radio.

That made every cop that was in pursuit of Bones become amped. When a cop hears the words "Shots fired," their adrenaline kicks in, and everybody becomes a super cop.

Bones had no idea where the shots came from. His heart skipped a beat when it went off. He was running out of gas. His lungs were burning and his legs were aching. At that moment, he regretted not hitting the gym. All he wanted to do was get out of the alleyway and get somewhere in the public eye. He thought it would be less likely that a cop would shoot an unarmed man in front of civilians.

"Get on the fuckin' ground. Get on the fuckin' ground," a cop yelled out with his gun pointed directly in Bones' face when he finally made it out of the alley.

Bones complied, falling to the ground right in front of the cop. He didn't give up because he wanted to, but because he had to. He was out of gas and couldn't run another second. He was actually kind of glad the chase was over, all the way up until one of the cops walked out of the alleyway with his gun. The first thing that came to his mind was that the gun the police just recovered was the same gun Isis used to kill Peanut and Fats.

Dave pulled into the park on 52nd Street on his motorcycle. He was supposed to be meeting up with Cees and Lump, but when he got there, only Lump was there, sitting on his bike. Saturday was their normal day to ride their bikes around the city, pretty much all day. Lump was happy to finally see his boy seeing as how he'd been missing in action for a couple of days. There was a lot Lump had to talk to him about with so little time to work with. He'd set up a plan with Isis to take Rita for everything she was worth, and at this time, Dave had no idea that he was spending quality time with someone who he may end up having to kill.

"Goddamn, playboy, whoever she is, she got a nigga whipped," Lump teased, seeing Dave get off his bike with a smile on his face.

What he said for the most part was true. Rita had his nose wide open, and he often found himself doing things with her that he usually wouldn't do with a woman that he just met. Growing up, Dave and Lump were something like pimps. For Lump to see his boy like this was funny.

"Cut it out. You know a nigga like me can't get whipped," he said, playing it off, taking a seat on the bench next to Lump. "So, what's good wit' dat situation? Is all the homework done on dat yet?"

"Yeah, man, and dis shit is sweet. The payoff look like it's going to be in the millions," Lump said, really catching Dave's attention.

Lump broke down just about everything he had thus far, and how they were supposed to be putting the plan in motion tomorrow. He told him about the situation that happened with Isis jumping in his car and how she was on some gangsta shit. Lump talked a mile a minute, and Dave could hardly keep up with everything he was saying. That's how Lump talked when he was excited. You would have had to have known him to understand him when he talked this way.

The one word he did hear perfectly clear through the whole conversation was the name Rita. When he heard Lump mention that name, he thought about the girl he'd been messing with. He only knew Rita by her real name, which was Sarita, and when he questioned Lump about the name, he only confirmed that the female he was talking about was named Rita and that he didn't know anybody named Sarita. As far as Lump was concerned, they were two different people.

"So, tomorrow we go to work?" Dave asked, kind of excited himself about the large amount of money that was involved.

"Yeah, man, tomorrow. So don't get lost, 'cause you know how much I hate to do a job without you, but I can't afford to let this opportunity pass," Lump shot back with the most serious look on his face Dave had ever seen.

Dave could see the sincerity in his eyes and knew for sure that it was definitely going down tomorrow. In a way, he was kind of happy because his money was starting to get low. Trying to keep up with Sarita was starting to take its toll. He was far from broke, but he was used to living a certain lifestyle and having a certain amount of money accessible to him at all times. Knowing that a lick was in the near future for a large amount of money took away a little stress for the most part.

For now, it was time to ride. The best part of being on a motorcycle was that it gave you a sense of freedom a car didn't offer. It was actually therapy for the both of them, and the only thing that was missing from today was Cees.

"What you got for me?" Isis asked, stepping to the side so that Matt could enter the house.

Ever since the shootout at the parking lot with Basco, Matt had supplied Isis with the cocaine they took. He only had access to about ten bricks, and they were just about gone. Isis was getting them for cheap, just as long as she kept Matt happy. That only took a shot of pussy and an occasional dick-suck. For that, she was only paying about 15k for each brick, five grand less than what she would normally have to pay from the average nigga in the streets. But even when it's good and you find somebody with low prices on coke, it never lasts forever.

"I got two for you, but I got to go up on the price because I'm getting down to my last," he replied, tossing the coke onto the living room table. "I need seventeen K, and I can't go no lower, baby girl. It'll get better in the future, I promise you."

Matt was starting to feel the effect of not only his drug, gambling, and tricking habits, but he was also seeing how Shay was starting to cut him off. Most of the $1.2 million they took from Basco went to Rita, and the couple hundred thousand they did have to spend, Matt was blowing it every day that went by, thinking that Rita was still going to break the rest of the money down. Rita was the boss, so she could have done whatever she wanted to do, breaking down the money any way she felt like. It was only by Shay that he got seven of the bricks to sell for himself. One shouldn't be surprised at how fast you can blow 100k, especially doing the things Matt was doing, and being as irresponsible as he was.

By any means, his loss was Isis's gain, and she only benefitted from him at a time when she needed it the most. It was pretty much because of Matt that Isis had more than one block to claim and was able to stack some money up. It was because of Matt that Isis had turned nothing into something, and he was so stupid and so blinded by her charm that he couldn't see that Isis didn't give two shits about him. He was only her steppingstone and an occasional good lay, that's it.

"So what's up wit' Shay?" Isis asked, walking up to him and wrapping her arms around his neck. "Did you think about what I asked you?"

"Man, I been told you. Me and Shay is just about over, so whatever you feel like you wanna do, just do it. Fuck, I want my money from dem bitches anyway," Matt said, thinking about all the money Rita had that he felt belonged to him.

"I'm glad you feel that way, because here's what I need you to do." She sat Matt down and got between his legs and took his dick out. In between kisses to his dick head, she told him her plan.

"I need you to get Shay alone." She kissed his dick head. "You've got to get her in a secluded place where there won't be any eyes. No cameras, nothing." Another kiss.

Matt was in ecstasy.

"She can't have no gun, so take her out for some romantic dinner. Tell her you want to make everything up to her, even though that's some bullshit, right?" She gave his dick a little suck. "When you're at dinner with her, you have to slip something in her drink. I'll supply you with this shit that'll knock her ass out good."

Matt was wit' it, gassed up wit' a full tank. Isis put the battery so far in his back he damn near ran up out of the house.

"Yo, one thing, though," Matt moaned. "Don't kill her. She don't deserve that."

Isis licked his dick head. "Anything you want, baby." She deep-throated him in one gulp.

Rita sat on her front steps, waiting for Dave to show up. She had her own plans for that night, instead of allowing Dave to keep taking over. She was at a point where she wanted to spend her own money, and for that matter, she wanted to spend some on Dave. It wasn't because she wanted to show off, nor because of the obvious fact that she was open, but it was more so to let Dave know that she was capable of pulling her own weight. She wanted Dave to know that she wasn't one of the average chickenheads out on the streets.

She looked down at her phone as it began to ring, thinking it was Dave calling to let her know that he was close by, but when Shay's number flashed across the screen, she was somewhat disappointed. She had to quickly come to her senses and realize this was her sister calling, someone who was more important than any nigga.

"Shay, what's up, baby girl?" she answered, still looking down the street for Dave's car to turn the block.

"ReRe, where have you been? I barely see you unless it's at home."

"That's something that I planned on talking to you about tomorrow," Rita told Shay, thinking about how she was ready to tell her about Dave.

"Bitch, you better not be pregnant," she joked, making Rita laugh at the thought.

Shay didn't have a clue about all the time Rita was spending with Dave and how much fun she was having. Rita didn't want to jinx anything and tell Shay about a man she just met, knowing that Shay wasn't going to approve of it. It wasn't that Shay controlled Rita's life concerning relationships, but they were sisters, and sisters who were close to one another like Shay and Rita always had an influence on each other's life when it came to boys.

"Big sis, I wasn't going to mention this to you right now, but I think you should hear this," Shay said, tuning down her voice in a more serious manner.

"Holla at me." Rita was hoping what Shay was about to say didn't ruin her day.

"Yo, word on the streets is that you're getting soft. The people don't see you out here no more, and they feel like we should have *been* retaliated for Peanut and Fats. The word is going around that Isis shot at us and she got us shook. Now, I'm not trying to do too much talking over this phone, but I think it's something that we need to address."

The news wasn't as bad as Rita thought it would be. It was more irritating than anything, considering all the work she'd put in so far throughout the hood. It's funny how some people forget. But even then, she respected the game, and every now and again, problems like this seemed to come up. The fix for it was easy, but the only problem Rita had and was at a disadvantage with was the fact that Isis was moving around more, so it was hard to catch up with her unless it was in traffic.

"Don't worry about that. I'ma take care of the chick as soon as I find out where she is," Rita said, referring to Isis.

"No! No! Her name is ringing bells over in Southwest. She supposed to have a couple of blocks out there. I just need the green light from you."

The brighter side of Rita's day turned down the block on his motorcycle, getting the attention of Rita and the few neighbors who were sitting outside. He looked so good, rocking a basic white t-shirt, some True Religion jeans, and a pair of Jordans.

Dave pulled right into the driveway, and for a moment, Rita almost forgot that Shay was on the phone. She had to admit, she was happy to see him.

"Everything's a go. Take care of that, then call me and let me know it's done," she said, hanging up the phone.

For Rita, it was just another executive call that she was used to making, but for Shay, it was a permit to wreak havoc on Isis and whatever part of the city she was in, something that was far past due. For now, Rita was trying to enjoy herself, as she'd been doing for the past week, something that she deserved.

"I got plans for us tonight for a change," she said, embarrassing Dave with a hug and a kiss on the cheek.

"You?" he asked with a shocked look on his face.

"Yeah, me. I made hotel arrangements at the Bailey's Casino in Atlantic City. I don't plan on doing no gambling, so don't give me any excuses about how you got to get some money. All you got to do is get in the car, and I'ma take care of the rest," she said, chirping the alarm on her car.

He couldn't do nothing but smile. She caught him off guard with this one, and she went even further by going into her pocket and pulling out a small jewelry box. She never forgot about the ring that he bought her on the first day they met. She was only returning the favor . . . times three.

"What's this?" he asked, grabbing the box out of her hand.

"Just a little somethin'-somethin' I picked up," she said, smiling.

When he opened the box, he put his head down, impressed with the gift she bought him. It was a watch. Not just any kind of watch. It was an Audemar, complete with a little ice around the bezel. He knew she had to have paid a pretty penny for it. He looked up at her and shook his head. Rita didn't understand that what she was doing was bigger than any amount she paid for the watch. She was making it hard for him to control his feelings for her.

Bones sat in the interrogation room, staring at the walls, trying to figure out why he didn't see the judge so that he could get bail. Just when he was about to get up and knock on the door, it opened, and in walked Detective Mozar. He tossed his folder on the table and took a seat right across from Bones. He had a look on his face that showed a sign of relief from running around all day.

"I guess you already know why I'm here," he said, leaning over to crack open his folder.

The moment Mozar spread out the pictures on the table, Bones knew he was hit. He didn't show it on the outside, but his heart started racing seeing Peanut, Fats, and crackhead Mike lying on the ground, dead. After getting himself together, he looked up at the detective like he didn't know who they were.

"What am I supposed to do wit' these?" he asked the detective, pushing the pictures back on his side of the table.

"Bones! Bones, Bones. You're going to learn that in life, we all make choices. Here, you got to make a choice for yourself, and to be honest with you, you only got one shot to do the right thing. After that, I promise you that I will make it so you won't ever see the streets again."

"Look, I don't know what you're talking about. My name—"

"Bones. Yeah, I know ya name," Mozar said, cutting him off. "And I guess you're going to tell me that the gun you got locked up with ain't have nothing to do with the murders."

"Like I said, I don't know what you're talking about."

"Yeah, for your sake, I hope you're telling me the truth, which I highly doubt," Mozar said, getting up from the table.

Chapter 13

Mozar walked into the park and headed for the swing set where Rita had told him to meet her. She was already waiting there for him, sitting on the end of the slide. Mozar was cautious, looking around every few seconds to make sure she was by herself. The first thing he did before any conversation could get started was pat-search Rita for any guns or wires. He was a cop, so he knew that anybody could be an informant, and taking the risk of being on audio was not in his plans for today.

"I didn't think you would come," Rita said, spitting out the sunflower seed shells she had in her mouth as Mozar patted her down.

"Yeah, well, I'm here. What do you want?" he asked as he continued to survey the premises.

"Straight to business. I like that," she said, sitting back down on the slide. "I been around the block long enough to know when somebody is trying to get me out of the way."

"Yeah, you got that right," Mozar responded with a smile on his face.

"My point exactly. So, it's pretty simple. You tell me who wants me gone, and I'll double whatever they are paying you."

Rita wasn't concerned about the money. She just wanted to know who was behind all the heat coming her way. Normally, niggas in the streets would try her by way of a gun, but whoever this was, they were trying to get her locked up. Jail was far worse than being dead in Rita's eyes, especially if the jail sentence lasted a lifetime.

"Well, you know that information is going to cost you," Mozar replied, pulling out a cigarette from his pocket.

"Whatever. Just talk."

"Hold up. Let's get something straight. I'm not ya average cop, so when you talk to me, you talk to me with some respect. It would mean nothing to me to put a bullet in ya head and go on about my day," he said, checking Rita's boss-like tone. "Now, when it comes to wanting to know who got it out for you, the best I could tell you is that it's somebody in ya camp. Somebody that's very close to you."

It was like a sharp pain that shot through Rita's chest when she heard that coming out of his mouth. She immediately started thinking about the people closest to her. There were only a handful of people in her immediate circle, and if Mozar was right about his source, it could only mean one of three people: Shay, Matt, Dave, or possibly Isis.

"I want a name," Rita demanded, curious as to who would betray her.

"I can't afford to tell you and then you go and kill him without me getting paid. You have ten K before the day is out, and I'll tell you exactly who it is."

"Ten K is a lot of money for one name. You better be providing a little more service than that," she responded, shocked at the number.

Rita had to think fast. She didn't want to miss out on this opportunity, and if she played her cards right, she could kill two birds with one stone. Mozar was a cop, but he was limited to what smarts he had of the streets. He was greedy, and greed always leads to failure.

"I got something even better for you. How about I direct you to a place where you and your partner can go and get fifty K and a few bricks of cocaine? You can keep the cash, and I'll buy the coke from you at street value."

"Enlighten me," he said, curious as to what she had in store.

Chapter 14

The sun was almost down, and there were still a lot of people hanging outside on 56th Street. It was business as usual, and now that Bones was locked up, Free had to step up and take control of the block. He was only going to do it until Bones got bailed out. The same workers worked the same shifts, and pretty much nothing else changed.

Free stood across the street from the Chinese store, watching as traffic picked up with the crackheads. It was a pretty young thing walking into the Chinese store that caught his eye, not even noticing where she came from. She had on knee-high boots, some blue Dereon jeans, and a cropped fitted t-shirt. On her face was a pair of Prada shades, something that just adds to a woman's beauty. In her hand was a Prada tote bag. He waited for her to come back out before he made his move, and once she did, he yelled out from across the street.

"Hold up, miss. Can I walk wit' you?" he asked, walking on the pavement next to her.

The girl smiled, knowing that he was going to say something to her. It would be damn near impossible for any man to resist saying something to her. As they continued to walk down the street, she listened to him kick his best game. In Free's eyes, this was probably the baddest chick he saw in this neighborhood, and he was curious as to where she was from.

"So, what's ya name?" he asked, stopping her at the top of the block.

"My name is Shay."

When he first heard the name Shay, he thought it sounded familiar, but the more he looked at her body, the more he didn't think about it. All he was pressed for was trying to get her number and hopefully get inside her panties before the night was over.

"Shay is a cute name. My name is Free. So, who do you know around here?"

When Shay heard his name, though, she quickly remembered one of the workers saying that he might have known one of the dudes that was with Isis when she set the house on fire. He said the guy looked like somebody named Free that was over Southwest all the time. He only knew that because he got around the city a lot.

"You might know my friend Isis. I was supposed to meet her on this block. She just moved around—"

"Yeah, yeah, I know Isis," he said, cutting her off. "She run dis block. She moved in that house over there," he told Shay, pointing to a house in the middle of the block. "She just left, though. If you want me to call her, I can do that," he said, reaching for the phone.

He was so caught up wit' trying to cater to Shay that he didn't notice the heavy flow of traffic slowing up. In fact, nothing was moving. It was like everything stopped. He didn't have any idea who he was talking to and the reason why she was there. He had no idea that Shay lured him off of the corner for one reason and one reason only. He was sitting in a blind spot, and if Chris, Dre, and Dog came up to the corner shooting while he was there, he would have had the drop on all of them.

By the time he'd noticed that everything was at a standstill, Chris, Dre, and Dog walked down on the corner from all angles and just started firing at everything moving. One of the workers tried to bend the corner in hopes of having a chance to pull his gun out, but Dre shot him in his back before he could turn the corner.

Free looked down the block and could see people running and falling on the ground, trying their best to get out of the way of the countless flying bullets. He could hear women screaming for their kids who were still outside playing, bullets hitting glass windows and parked cars. The sounds of screeching tires speeding down the street flooded the air, and what was once a Chinese store was now riddled with bullets.

Free didn't know what was going on and as he looked down the street. He could only see the sparks spitting out of one of the gunmen's hands and people taking cover behind cars. Feeling the vibe of it being a set-up, he reached in his waist and grabbed his gun, pulling it out before he turned back around to Shay.

Now, remembering the name Shay from Isis telling him about her, he felt a sense of fear. If he had remembered who she was from the beginning, he would have shot her the moment he saw her, but his memory processed the information too late, and the later for him was better for Shay. The gun was out of her Prada bag and pointed straight at his face as he turned around. He had the dumb look on his face as though he knew he fucked up and trying to raise his gun to shoot Shay was pointless.

Shay blew him a kiss before she pulled the trigger, damn near knocking his head off of his shoulders with a single shot. Shay speed-walked down the street to the Chinese store where, on the ground, lay the worker Chris shot in his back and the other worker who was shot in his stomach. Chris, Dre, and Dog had already retreated to their car, so Shay was all alone. She walked up to the corner and stood over the worker who was shot in the stomach, kicking him in his side so that he would look up at her.

"Give Isis a message for me," she said, pointing the gun six inches from his face. She closed her eyes and squeezed the trigger, knocking a chunk of meat out of his forehead, killing him instantly. In the distance, she could hear cop sirens, and as she walked off the corner, she put two more bullets in the worker who was shot in the back.

Her antics were more than just wanting to shoot up Isis's block. She wanted to really send Isis a message, and that message was: "It's on."

Shay calmly walked around the corner and got into her car, waiting for Chris, Dre and Dog to pull up beside her, which they did within seconds. When the smoke had cleared, three of Isis's workers were shot and killed, and her block was hot as fish grease with the cops. Fifty-sixth Street was definitely going to be shut down for a while, and that by itself was a blow Isis couldn't afford right now. The sun wasn't even down, and it was still going to be a long night. When Shay got a green light to go, it wasn't going to stop until everything was flatlined.

"Brian Hopkins!" the guard yelled into the bullpen, looking for Bones.

Finally, he thought to himself, ready to see the judge for a bail hearing. He wanted to hurry up and make bail before the detective had enough time to do a ballistics report on the gun. Trying to bail out after that would have been the last thing on his mind.

The guard pulled him out of the bullpen and directed him back to the same interview room he was in six hours ago. Detective Mozar and another man in a suit were sitting in the room. He had a feeling what was about to go down. Bones stood in the corner of the room with his back to the wall. He didn't want to take a seat.

"I think you might want to sit down, Mr. Hopkins," Mozar said, breaking the silence in the room.

"Standing up, sitting down, what's the difference?" he shot back.

"You know, I'm disappointed in you. I thought that you were a smarter person than that. I hope you didn't think that I wasn't going to do the ballistics report on the gun you got locked up with. You lied to me, Bones," Mozar said, sliding the ballistics report across the table.

Bones was feeling like Cane from *Menace II Society,* when the detective told Cane in the interrogation room, "You know you done fucked up, right?" It was then Bones decided that it was time to take a seat. Thinking about the judge saying the words "life without parole" made his legs feel like noodles. He pulled the papers closer to him so that he could read them as the ballistics officer who Mozar brought with him began to explain what he was looking at.

"Now look, Bones. You can help yourself in this situation, and I can talk to the D.A. and make sure that you don't spend the rest of your life in jail," Mozar chimed in. "I know you didn't do this all by yourself, so just give us a name."

Bones sat there thinking about what Mozar was saying, but he also thought about what he would become if he did what Mozar was asking him to do. He would become a rat, and being a rat was the worst thing you could become in the criminal world. He would never be able to hold his head up and honestly say that he was a man. Real men stand on what they do and take full responsibility for their actions, even when the end result of that action means the possibility of having to do time in prison. One should never bring down the next man because you fucked up and got caught.

The room got quiet, and not a word was being said by either the detectives or by Bones. He looked as though he was going to hold up and stand his ground. Besides, the only evidence they had was the gun. They weren't even able to place him at the scene of the crime. That was enough for Bones to keep his mouth shut.

The ballistics expert continued his presentation. "So, as I was saying, you can see the markings on the bullets match the pattern produced by this exact gun. The gun that was found on you. Therefore, we are certain this gun was used in the murders of the three bodies found previously."

"There you have it, Bones." Mozar smiled. "We have enough evidence for a jury to convict. You can't argue with this type of slam dunk proof. Have fun doing life." Mozar turned to the ballistics expert. "I think we're done here."

The ballistics expert gathered his papers. Mozar waited for him and acted like Bones wasn't even there. Once the ballistics expert was ready, they both headed for the exit.

"Wait," Bones said before Mozar closed the door behind him.

Mozar paused and looked at Bones. "Yes?"

"Let's talk," Bones said.

It was coming up on midnight, and it had just started to rain by the time Shay pulled into her driveway. She'd had a long day, and from somebody who didn't know any better, one might think that she was coming home from an honest 9 to 5 job. Her hair was sweated out, and her clothes look like she'd been jogging in a marathon. She was tired and hungry, and even though she didn't feel like dealing with Matt's bullshit, she wondered where he was, not seeing his car in the driveway.

After leaving 56th Street, Shay had attempted to shake down another street that she believed belonged to Isis.

Unfortunately, Isis wasn't there. Shay had waited out there for almost two hours, hoping she would show her face, but she never came. In fact, Shay never really got a chance to find out whether 59th Street belonged to Isis. When she got there, the niggas there weren't playing games. They were used to people trying to rob them, and they definitely weren't going for the cute-girl-in-a-nice-outfit scheme. What looked like an easy shakedown quickly turned into a full-fledged shootout within seconds.

Shay and her squad casually turned the corner to walk down the block. The moment they turned, all the boys on the block turned to look at them. At first, Shay thought they were all thirsty for a shot of pussy, but she quickly realized that wasn't the case. As soon as she saw several of them reach for their guns, she knew it was about to get hectic. They fired on Shay and her squad before they got a chance to make it all the way down the block.

Everyone scattered the moment shots rang out. The crackheads screamed and ran, the dope boys all took cover. Shay and her squad jumped behind some parked cars and unloaded their clips on the dope boys. Shay popped her head up to find someone to shoot at, and before she had time to focus her eyes, a bullet whizzed past her ear. She ducked down faster than a clam retreating into its shell.

Shay looked at her crew, all squatting behind the car. There was no need to say anything, Shay stood up and sprayed bullets as her crew ran away. Shay, in high-heel boots, ran backward as she shot at the dealers.

That was the last stop of the day for Shay. She'd had enough of the chase for one day. She needed to regroup and get back to it the next day.

Shay walked up her driveway toward the front door, and suddenly the hairs on the back of her neck stood up.

She immediately reached into her bag for her gun, but by the time her hand touched the butt of it, she could see a gunman walking from behind the garage, pointing a shotgun directly at her face. Lump came from the side of the house, pointing an additional two Glock 9 mm at her. Looking through the rain, she found it hard to get a visual of the faces, so she didn't have any idea who it was.

"Don't be stupid and get yaself killed," Cees said, easing up to her with the shotgun in his hands.

He could see that Shay still had her hand in her pocketbook, and from the way she stared them down, he knew that this abduction wasn't going to be as easy as they hoped it would be.

Shay quickly calculated the distance between her and Lump, who came from behind the house, which was about forty feet away, and then she did the same for Cees. He was only a mere fifteen feet away. She looked around as far as she could see, to see if anybody else was with them, but there wasn't anyone else.

Pulling the gun from her bag would take up too much time, so Shay gripped the gun tighter, pointing it in the direction of Cees, who had the shotgun. She began squeezing the trigger. Bullets ripped through the Prada bag and headed straight for Cees, who managed to get off a single buck-shot before retreating back behind the garage.

Shay began back-pedaling while she continued to fire, but she couldn't catch her grip in the slippery grass. Lump fired several shots at Shay's legs, not wanting to kill her. She would have been no good to him dead. He hit her twice in one leg and once in the other. She fell to the ground, whipping the gun out of her pocketbook so that she could get a better shot. The rain falling in her eyes made it harder to focus. She fired her last three shots in the direction of Lump. She got lucky and hit him once in his left arm. The other two bullets lodged into the house.

Lump ignored the pain of the bullet wound and kept advancing on Shay. He heard the gun click, which told him she was out of bullets. He stood over her, ready to blow her face off. He was pissed that she had shot him. He could feel his arm throbbing where the bullet went through.

"I can't believe this bitch shot me."

Cees came from behind the garage, looking at the lights of the neighbors' houses starting to come on. Shay looked up at Lump, who was standing over her with the gun in her face. It was the last thing she saw before Cees knocked her over the head with the butt of the shotgun and knocked her out.

Chapter 15

"Search Warrant! Search Warrant!" SWAT agents yelled out, breaking down Isis's front door with the battering ram. They entered the house with guns out. They went from room to room, searching for Isis, who was now wanted for a triple homicide. She was considered armed and extremely dangerous, so police wouldn't hesitate to put a bullet in her melon if she decided to jump out of one of these rooms with a gun, even though she was a female.

"Clear," the officers yelled after searching each room.

She wasn't in the house, but she sure left behind a lot of incriminating evidence. Mozar led the search of the house, and during that time, he uncovered a large amount of cocaine, baggies, scales, ammunition for several different guns, and in her bedroom, Mozar found a 9 mm Beretta, the same kind of gun used in the murders.

Bones couldn't hold water. Not only did he confess to being at the murder scene, but he made Isis and Free out to be the shooters. He played the role like he was just there to rob them, but Isis and Free went crazy while they were in there. He thought about all that ratting stuff, but it went out the door the moment his gun came back as one of the guns involved in the shooting. They didn't even have any evidence besides the gun, but now, they had a full, legally obtained confession. He was no different than the guy on the show called *The First 48*. He started off strong but ended up folding when a little bit of pressure was applied.

Mozar stood on Isis's front porch, looking up and down 56th Street, noticing yellow tape surrounding certain areas of the block. Due to his adrenaline pumping because of the warrant for Isis, he didn't notice the crime scene that was already in progress.

"What happened here?" he asked one of the officers working the scene.

"We had a triple homicide out here last night. The shooter executed all three at point blank range," the officer informed him.

"Point blank?" Mozar asked, shocked.

"Yeah, and witnesses say that it was a female who finished off the two guys on the corner. The guy at the other end of the block might have been shot with the same gun. We're waiting for the ballistics to come back."

The officer walked Mozar through a more extensive tour of the crime scene, breaking down all possible theories of the chain of events that had happened the night before. Mozar had a gut feeling that this case was connected with the case he was investigating. Some detectives had that kind of sixth sense when it came to solving cases. Even though he wasn't sure, he made it his business to take down some notes for further analysis.

Shay woke up with a headache, finding herself handcuffed to a large radiator that sat in the living room of an unfamiliar house. She could hear the sounds of footsteps upstairs and the low voices of her captors talking amongst each other. Things were still a little blurry, but she could clearly see that the house she was in was nice. It had a fifty-inch flat screen TV up against the wall, the sofa and love seat were real leather, and the carpet was the thick expensive kind. She could smell food coming from the kitchen, and out of the blue, a little girl appeared, coming down the steps. It was freaking Shay out, and she thought about calling out to the people upstairs, but she didn't have to. They were making their way downstairs.

Not to her surprise, coming down the steps was Cees, the one whom she remembered quite well from the blow she took to her head. Of course, he looked different than he had in the rain with a shotgun pointed at her. He was followed by Lump, who had a patch on his arm from the bullet Shay grazed him with. She only wished that it was his head instead of his arm. The shocker came when Isis walked down the steps, clutching a chrome .45 in her hand with a big smile on her face. She tucked the gun away in her waistband and picked up the little girl at the end of the steps.

"I want you to meet somebody," Isis said to the little girl, who was too young to understand what was going on. "I want you to meet your cousin. Her name is Shay-Shay. Say hi to Shay-Shay," Isis told the little girl who was too shy to say anything.

Lump grabbed a chair out of the dining room and placed it right in front of Shay. He didn't waste any time smacking the shit out of her, just to get some understanding about what was going on here. He smacked her so hard it almost knocked her back out.

"What da fuck do y'all want?" Shay asked, spitting blood out of her mouth.

She could see Isis walking away into the kitchen as though she didn't want to see this part of the interrogation, knowing that it was about to get ugly if Shay didn't cooperate. Cees didn't pay too much mind either, flicking through the channel like he was waiting for his favorite TV show to come on. Lump quickly got her attention again with another smack.

"You can make this easy on yourself, and I give you my word that you will live through this. But if you lie to me and act like you don't know what I'm talking about, I promise you that I'm going to kill you in the worst way. Then I'm going to kill your sister, and then I'ma kill your grandma Mrs. Scott," Lump said, lifting her chin up so that she could see him. "Now, what did your sister do with the money and the coke y'all took from Basco?"

"I don't know what you're talking about," Shay said, spitting out another glob of blood.

Lump smacked her again, this time to the point where he did knock her out. Cees looked at Lump, who had a dumb look on his face like he didn't expect her to do that. That's why Dave always did the interrogation part of a kidnapping or home invasion. Lump didn't know his own strength, and now he had to find a way to wake her up again to get what he wanted.

"Look, I told you, you don't have to go through all of that to get the money. Trust me," Isis said, coming out of the kitchen, seeing Shay knocked out again. "Somebody give me a phone."

Rita and Dave lay in the bed, looking out of the window at the ocean. It was beautiful. Last night was amazing. They went to a show, had a nice dinner, walked the boardwalk, and even played the slot machines for a while. The sex was incredible and different than the other times they engaged in it. It was more sensual. It had more meaning, and if Rita didn't know any better, she could have sworn that Dave made love to her. At least that's the way it felt.

Rita was having the time of her life, and every time she got with Dave, pretty much nothing concerning the streets mattered. He was like her escape from the reality of her everyday life she wished she was never born into. What woman wakes up and decides that she wants to be a gangsta? It was something that ran through her blood. For Rita, it was the only way she knew how to live since she was a child. She didn't live this life because she wanted to, but because she was bred this way. At the right time and with the right man in her life, she had plans on getting out of the game, with dreams of living the most normal life she could.

The life she wanted was farther down the road than she thought. As long as she was a boss in the streets, something was always bound to come up, and at times, even bosses had to get their hands dirty.

The sound of her phone ringing dampened the mood, breaking the tranquility she and Dave were sharing, spooning completely naked in the bed. She wasn't going to answer it, and at first she didn't, but whoever was trying to call her was persistent. They called the phone three times before Rita decided to answer it.

"Whaaaaaaat," she answered, seeing that it was Matt.

"Yo, they got her, Rita. They got my baby," he cried into the phone.

"What, what? Wait. Slow down. What do you mean somebody got her? Got who?" Rita said, sitting up in the bed.

"Somebody kidnapped Shay. They called here saying they want money. Ohhhh God," Matt cried out.

Rita's heart dropped. She hung up the phone immediately and jumped out of the bed. Dave didn't know what was going on, but he knew something was wrong, so without saying a word, he jumped out of bed and began getting dressed too. Within minutes, they were both out the door and headed to the elevator. Rita fumbled trying to get her phone out of her pocket to call Matt back, wanting to make sure he wasn't playing around. Shit, if he was playing around, Rita probably would have killed him, literally. She couldn't dial the number any quicker, speeding off the elevator and into the parking lot with Dave in tow.

"Matt, did they say what they wanted?" Rita yelled into the phone, struggling to keep her reception in the parking lot.

"Money! They said they want money," he yelled back into the phone.

Rita hung up the phone, thinking something wasn't right. She couldn't figure out or understand why somebody would kidnap Shay. She was getting some money, but anybody that knew Shay had to know Rita, and if that was the case, they knew Rita was worth more if somebody was to be kidnapped.

She started running to the car when she saw it in the parking lot. Before she could stick her key in the door, Dave stopped her. She had almost forgotten Dave was with her. He grabbed a hold of her before she could get the door opened, remembering that they both had guns in the car and speeding through Atlantic City would get you pulled over quick.

"Let me drive," he demanded, giving her a stern look as though he wasn't going to take no for an answer. "At the rate you're going, we're not going to make it home. Whatever is going on, it's going to be there when we get there."

"They kidnapped Shay," Rita cried out, feeling the seriousness of what was going on.

It was all starting to come together. Rita was realizing that Shay wasn't the intended target. It was her. It was the lack of being out in the streets that prevented the kidnappers from grabbing Rita, but in a sense, it made it easier to grab the closest thing to her, which was Shay.

Rita immediately started blaming herself for what was going on. She could hardly stand on her own two feet after thinking about the possibility of Shay being shot in her head by the kidnappers. She broke down in tears, falling into Dave's arms, something he never saw her do and never wanted to see her do again.

Without a question, Dave was there to comfort her, hugging her and confirming that everything was going to be all right. In the back of his mind, he had a feeling that it wasn't, considering his experience in the field of kidnapping.

"I'm definitely driving," he said, walking her around to the passenger side.

"We have breaking news this afternoon coming out of West Philadelphia," the news anchor announced over the television.

Shay cracked open her eyes once again, only to see Isis's face all over the midday news. Cees was sitting on the couch, staring into the TV, while he munched down on something he had cooked in the kitchen. The little girl that she saw earlier was asleep on the couch next to him. Shay could barely hear what was being said by the news anchor, but she could clearly see the "wanted" sign underneath Isis's name.

"The suspect is considered armed and extremely dangerous. Apparently, police officials say that this woman, Shannel Thompkins, was involved in a triple homicide in West Philadelphia last week. One suspect is already in custody. Police are urging people not to go near Ms. Thompkins if you see her. Just call the police. We'll be back to this story in just a few," the news anchor reported, and then changed over to the weatherman.

Shay couldn't believe what she just saw. It even blew Cees' mind watching that come over the news like that, and for a minute, he debated whether to go upstairs and tell Lump and Isis to turn on the TV.

Cees looked over his shoulder to see that Shay was awake. He quickly got up and attended to her, feeling kind of bad about Lump hitting her the way he had. He wasn't sweet or soft for feeling this way, but he admired the loyalty she had for her sister. And even looking at the possibility of being tortured and killed wasn't enough to break her. It takes a lot for anybody to be strong in the situation she was in, and for that, he gave Shay a bit of respect.

"Are you hungry?" he asked, lifting up the burger he had in his hand. "I can make you one of these."

Hunger pangs had kicked in, but Shay wasn't about to trust Cees with getting her something to eat, especially food she couldn't watch him prepare in front of her. It didn't matter that he was trying to be nice to her. Shay wasn't trusting anybody.

"Look, dis shit ain't personal, baby girl. It's business," Cees said, raising her head up to look her in the eyes. "I know it look ugly right now, but it'll get greater later," he said, standing up to walk away.

"Why me?" Shay asked, stopping him in his tracks, hoping to get an answer.

Cees ignored her question and walked off into the kitchen. Shay could hear a pot being placed on the stove and the sound of water running. She could also hear loud music coming from upstairs and the faint sound of a woman moaning in the background.

"Oooohhhhhh, ssshhiiit," Isis screamed out, looking back at Lump pounding away from the back. She held on to the headboard, throwing her ass back at Lump as he shoved his long, thick dick deeply inside of her juice box. Her round, soft ass clapped up against his pelvic bone, and her titties bounced up and down to the rhythm and motion.

He rested one hand on top of her ass, while wrapping the other around her thigh. Isis's pussy was on 1000, and as Lump continued to deep stroke, he could feel her cum dripping down his balls and onto the bed. He fucked so hard that the patch on his arm fell off. The stinging sensation from the deep gash didn't faze him one bit, nor did it mess with his performance.

Aggressively, he flipped Isis over on her back, spreading her legs wide apart to get a good look at what was making him feel so good. Isis looked up at him, biting her bottom lip seductively, motioning with her fingers for Lump to slide inside of her. He did, but not before slapping his dick against her clit a few times, making her jump a little. He grabbed a handful of her titties, leaned over, and went back inside of her.

She moaned as his thickness entered her womb, holding onto his back, pulling him closer down to her face so that she could kiss him.

"Deeper. Go deeper," she whispered in his ear, kissing the side of his neck and swaying her body to his motion. "Harder, Lump," she moaned, digging her nails into his shoulders.

Without a condom, he could feel her warm, wet, soft insides as he dug deep enough to hit her back wall. He tried to hold back, but he couldn't. He tried to think about sports, but it wasn't working. Her pussy was too good, and the more she came all over Lump's dick, the more sensitive it felt. He was exploding, and there was no way he was pulling out. Isis didn't seem to want him to anyway, pulling him closer as his facial expression told the tale of him getting ready to cum.

She felt his warm liquid oozing inside of her, bringing her to the point of climax as well. Their bodies began to shiver at the same time, and Isis held on for dear life, squirting her sweet juices all over Lump's dick. He even felt it splashing on his stomach.

She stared at Lump, unable to feel her legs. As she basked in enjoyment, she couldn't help but to wonder how she got to this point.

Everything had happened so fast. She was attracted to Lump the moment she met him, and it wasn't till a couple of days ago that Lump started coming around discussing more than just business. One thing led to another, and everything else was history. Isis found herself being somewhat of a girlfriend within days, a title she didn't really mind having, just as long as Matt would fall back and respect the game.

Chapter 16

Hearing Rita's car pulling up in the driveway, Matt managed to work up a few tears to go along with the sad look he had on his face. He had to make it look as real as possible, or else Rita would see right through him. She was good at spotting a fake, but being in this type of situation, Rita could easily miss the obvious. Matt knew he had to put on his A game. His life was depending on it.

"Maaat," Rita yelled, coming through the front door, gun in hand and Dave in tow.

"I'm right here," he said, coming from out of the kitchen with the house phone in his hand.

"What the hell is goin' on, and who da fuck got Shay?" she questioned, looking at Matt with the most curious look on her face.

"I don't know yet. They said they were going to call back at two o'clock. I'm just waiting for the call."

"What did they say? When did it happen? Where were you? How many niggas was it that took her? Who saw it happen? Anyone? Did she fight back?" Rita asked questions without waiting for answers.

Matt was already a suspect in Rita's eyes, and maybe the reason for it was that she was upset somebody took Shay. Shay was like her world. She was Rita's baby sister, and she had told her dad that she was going to look out for her. Now, the promise she stood by for all these years was being broken on account of Rita neglecting her duties as a responsible guardian. It was eating her up with every second that went by that Shay didn't come walking through the front door.

Looking up at the clock, Rita saw that she had a little less than one hour until the kidnappers called back. She ran upstairs to see how much money she had on hand, along with cocaine, just in case she had to negotiate a ransom. If it came down to it, she would give up every-thing she had to get Shay back, even the money she had still tied up in the streets. It would be easy for Rita to start over from ground zero, but it was better than stayin' rich having to bury her sister.

"So, how did you find out that Shay was kidnapped?" Dave asked Matt, trying to get some understanding while Rita was upstairs.

Dave found it funny that Matt's body language wasn't adding up to the standards of a man who just found out his girl was kidnapped. There wasn't a specific way a man should act, but Matt wasn't showing too many signs of anything. He was too calm, and every time Rita said something, he'd put his head down like he couldn't stand to look her in the face. It just tingled Dave's spider senses and made him more curious as to what was going on.

"I don't know. They just called and said, 'We got ya bitch, nigga,' and I thought it was somebody playin' on my phone, so I hung up. Then they called right back, and I could hear Shay in the background screaming my name. I asked them what they wanted, and they said money."

"How do you know that it was Shay screaming in the background?" Dave asked, seeing that he left out the part about hearing Shay in the background when he was tell-ing Rita what happened.

"I don't know. I mean, I think it was her. I mean it sounded like her," Matt said, stuttering with every other word that came out of his mouth.

Dave had robbed too many people, so many times, and he knew the character of the one being preyed upon. He could sense that Matt was either lying about something or leaving out something he knew. He might have been able to pull the wool over Rita's eyes because she was too upset at the moment, but for a pair of fresh eyes like Dave's, it was impossible for Matt to convince him that he didn't have more information about his girlfriend, the one whom he said he loved so much.

If he loved her so much, he wouldn't be sitting there waiting for another phone call. The first phone call would have been enough to get the price of the ransom, what time and place the transaction would take place, and where he could pick Shay up. Kidnappers normally have these types of things mapped out before they do the actual kidnapping; that is, unless they were rookies and didn't know any better, which also could be the case.

"Did you ever try calling Shay's phone?" Dave asked, pulling up a chair at the dining room table where Matt was sitting.

"Naw, I didn't," Matt replied, beginning to feel a little uncomfortable with Dave's deposition. "In fact, dog, who da hell are you to be asking all these fucking questions about my bitch?" Matt snapped back, feeling like Dave was interrogating him. "You—"

"Hold up, hold up, hold up. Pump ya mafuckin' brakes, nigga. I don't know Shay, but I know Rita, and that's who I'm here for. You got a fuckin' problem wit' dat, then do something," Dave said, standing to his feet with his fists clenched.

Matt stood to his feet too, not being a stranger to a good ole fisticuff. They squared off in the dining room, but before a punch could be thrown, Rita came running down the steps, hearing the commotion from her room. There was a little hesitation by Rita getting in between them. She hesitated seeing Dave look over top of Matt like he was about to pound on him. It was a look she had never seen on Dave's face, but she knew he had a gorilla inside of him. Initially, it shocked her, but she liked it, feeling a sense of security that Dave wouldn't let anything happen to her.

"Whoa, whoa, whoa," she yelled, jumping in between them before the punches started to fly. "Now, everybody needs to calm down. Matt, you take a walk," Rita said, pointing to the front door. "Dave, you—"

Dave's phone ringing cut Rita off. He almost didn't realize it was ringing himself, keeping his eyes on Matt as he walked out the front door. His mind was set on fighting or doing whatever else Matt wanted to do. Rita called his name twice, snapping him out of his trance. He looked down at his phone to see that it was Lump calling him. Today was the day he was supposed to put in his work with Lump and Cees, and with everything that was going on with Rita, he had forgotten about it.

"I got to take this call," he said, walking away from Rita and going into the kitchen. "Yo, what's good, Cannon?" he answered, knowing what Lump wanted already.

"Damn, nigga, I been tryin' to call you all night. I went on and made that move already last night. I need to holla at you asap."

Lump really needed Dave. He wasn't the negotiating type. He had already kidnapped, smacked, and knocked Shay out, and she still wasn't talking. He tried to use Dave's tactics of threatening, but even that didn't work. With Lump, Shay would never give up the money, and he definitely wasn't skillful enough to negotiate a ransom.

"Meet me at my crib in twenty minutes," Dave told Lump, looking off into the living room at Rita staring out the window. His mind was racing a million miles per second thinking about how coincidental it was that

Lump made his move last night and Shay was missing since last night.

Maybe it's just a coincidence, he thought to himself, walking back into the living room. He walked up behind Rita and wrapped his arms around her waist.

"He didn't mean no harm," she said, referring to Matt, who she watched walk back and forth outside.

"Don't worry about it. I can understand his frustration. Look at me," he said, turning Rita around to face him. "We're gonna get her back. You hear me?" he said, lifting her chin up. "I got to go take care of something real quick. I'll be back in about an hour. I want you to call my phone as soon as the kidnappers call you. You got me?"

She nodded her head in compliance.

Dave looked out the window at Matt. He didn't trust him that much, and he didn't feel comfortable leaving Rita alone with him, but he didn't have a choice. It was time for him to go to work, and Lump was waiting for him. He just had to make it back as soon as possible.

"All right, everybody. Can I have your attention?" Detective Mozar announced, standing in front of a classroom full of cops.

Isis's picture was as big as day on the chalkboard behind him, sitting on top of a pyramid of evidence. She was Philly's most wanted, and the tactical team Mozar put together was running up in any house they thought Isis might be in. Today was just a briefing before they kicked down two more doors at places she was known to have been living in at one point. Not only was she a suspect in the triple homicide in West Philly, but she was now wanted for questioning in the triple homicide in Southwest Philly as well.

"If you don't already know, Chanel Thompkins, AKA Isis, is wanted for a triple homicide and possibly was involved in a separate triple homicide that occurred last night," Mozar said, pointing at the pyramid on the chalkboard. "Nine out of ten, she has a gun, and by the looks of things, she's not afraid to use it. In fact, I believe she prefers to use it, so don't hesitate to put a bullet in her head if she even blinks the wrong way. We want to take her alive, if possible, but if it comes to her life or yours, well, I guess nothing else has to be said. Let's suit up and catch the bad girl," Mozar declared, rallying up his troops.

Shay looked down at her legs. They hurt like hell, and she could feel the bullets inside of them. She needed medical attention bad because she had lost a lot of blood overnight. Cees ripped up a sheet and tied up her legs, but that wasn't enough. She could easily get infected with gangrene and her legs would have to be amputated if the wounds weren't attended to properly.

"Take these," Cees said, walking over to Shay with a couple of pills and a bottle of water. "It's penicillin and Motrin. It will help ya legs from getting infected and hopefully ease some of the pain. It shouldn't be much longer now," he said, placing the pills in her mouth, then the water.

For some odd reason, Cees had been nice to Shay throughout the whole process. He even apologized for knocking her upside the head with his gun. In a way, he felt sorry for Shay, watching her go through everything she was going through and suffering through the wounds she had. After being around her and having extensive conversations with her, he saw that she wasn't too bad a person at all.

"Your friend is going to kill me after y'all get the money, isn't he?" Shay asked, looking up at Cees with puppy-dog eyes.

"Ah, listen, I give you my word that nobody's going to kill you," he said, looking back at her with a sincere look in his eyes. "I think you've been through enough, but at the same time, you have to give me your word that you won't kill me if you ever see me on the streets," he said in a joking way, but he was as serious as a heart attack.

Through all that she'd been through, Shay managed to crack a smile at Cees' joke. She didn't know why, but for some reason, she believed and trusted that he would keep his word. What he asked in return for his word was asking for a lot, but it was also manageable considering that he could guarantee her life after it was all over with.

"I give you my word," she shot back with the same serious look Cees gave her.

Dave pulled up and parked in front of his house. Lump was already there waiting for him, sitting in his car across the street. Dave walked over to his car and motioned for Lump to get out so they could walk and talk. Lump jumped out of his car with a little extra spunk, excited about the news he had for Dave. It wasn't long before Lump started breaking down the stats on the situation, and the more he talked, the more things started to come together.

"Yo, so I was tryin' to track you down, but you was AWOL," Lump said.

"Yeah, nigga, so what. I told you I'd be ready."

"I know. It was now or never, though. See, I was looking for Rita, but this chick Isis got in the way. She was on some shit about helping us get to Rita through her girl Shay. She also had Shay boyfriend, this nigga Matt, who gonna help wit' it all," Lump said. "You see, I had to pull the trigger and set this bitch Shay up quick."

Dave shook his head. He was in disbelief.

"So, now we got this bitch, and we supposed to make a call at two o'clock to set up payment. But get this. This nigga Matt say that Rita be dating a nigga who be getting a lot of money in the city, and we can add him to the mix. This is gonna be a huge payday, nigga."

It blew Dave's mind when Lump said that Shay's boyfriend was going to help them get Rita next. He wanted to tell Lump to call everything off and let Shay go, but it was a little too late. Everything was in progress, and Lump wasn't the type to abort a mission, especially halfway through it. Plus, Lump was his boy, and it would be hard to cross him over a female he just met a couple of weeks ago. He had to think of something. Most importantly, he had to hurry up and get back to Rita because she was at home, alone with Matt.

"Yo, you sure about dis chick? 'Cause I got a lick lined up right now that's worth some real money," Dave said, using this as his final attempt to get Lump not to go through with it.

"Man, fuck dat. These bitches got cake, bro. It's easy money, and I already grabbed one of them. Nigga, I hope you ain't getting soft on me," Lump joked, throwing a punch at Dave.

"Naw, nigga, ain't shit soft about me. I just don't wanna be wasting my time wit' no bullshit. I got better shit to do wit' my time than to be playing around wit' some bitches."

Dave was trying, but Lump wasn't budging. He had his target locked and loaded, and at this point, there wasn't anything or anybody who could change that. He was on this one, and if Dave wasn't tryin' to move out, then he damn sure was going to make it happen on his own. It might get a little messier than he hoped, but all in all, it was going down.

"So, is you in, nigga?" Lump asked, waiting to hear Dave's final answer.

Decisions, decisions, Dave thought to himself. How do you choose between a friend you've known all your life and a girl you just met two weeks ago? The answer should be easy for the average nigga in the streets, but for Dave, it wasn't quite that simple. This was the first time in his life that he had met a girl he connected with on a level beyond any measure. He had no idea when or if this chance would ever come back again, and at the same time, he made a blood in blood oath with his best friend to stay loyal to one another. Lump would never understand the way Dave felt about Rita, especially at this point in time. Dave honestly didn't know what he was going to do, but he knew he had to give Lump an answer.

"Don't feed her, don't give her a drink of water, don't talk to her, and definitely don't make that phone call at two o'clock. I'ma take care of some business, and I'll call you in two hours. Oh, and make sure you put her in the basement, cover all the windows, and turn off all the lights so she can't see shit. I want to make this shit quick and as easy as possible," Dave instructed, heading back to his car.

Chapter 17

The house phone ringing caught Rita and Matt's attention, and for a second, Rita hesitated answering it, fearing the worst. Her heart was racing, and as much as she saw these types of situations happen on TV, it was nothing like the real thing. Matt even offered to answer it, seeing that she was hesitant. She refused, clicking the talk button on the phone.

"Hello," she answered, trying to be as calm as she could.

"Sarita, the police just came busting down my door, looking for dat girl," Grandma Scott yelled into the phone. "Now, I don't know what dat girl did, but I told the police she didn't live here, and they still searched this house top to bottom. I don't live like this, Sarita. I'm too old. My front door broke, and one of dem sumbitches almost knocked me over."

"What girl?" Sarita asked

"Chanel. They came here looking for Chanel." Ms. Scott was giving Rita an earful.

Rita had never heard her grandmother get so upset, and as bad as she wanted to stay on the phone and find out what was going on with Isis, it had just turned 2:00.

"Grandma, Grandma, I'ma call you right back. Let me find out what's going on," Rita said, not wanting to, but hanging up on her.

Rita wondered what in the hell Isis did to have the cops running in her grandmother's house. No more than twenty seconds went by, and Matt was calling Rita back into the living room, pointing at the TV. Isis's face was taking up the whole screen. The news anchor reported the same story she did that afternoon, but this time, a reward for her capture was posted by the Philadelphia police department. Ten thousand dollars, to be exact. Rita sat there with her mouth wide open as the news anchor continued with the story.

The sound of her car pulling up in the driveway took her attention away from the TV. Dave was back, and by the look he had on his face walking through the door, Rita knew that something was wrong. She thought that he still might be mad at Matt about the situation that happened before he left, so when Dave pulled his gun from out of his back pocket, Rita walked up on him. Matt was so into the news that he didn't even realize what was going on.

Dave looked Rita in her eyes as she stood inches from his face. "Just trust me," Dave said, placing his hand on her waist and moving her to the side.

Rita's body went from being tense to being at ease. She stepped to the side and let Dave do what he did. He picked the remote control up off the edge of the couch and turned the TV off. That's when Matt finally looked up to see Dave standing before him with a gun in his hand. Matt looked at his gun, which was about five feet away, sitting on the table in front of him, and for a moment, he thought about grabbing it.

"I'll empty this whole clip out on you before you get to it," Dave assured Matt, giving him a look to try it.

"Nigga, you gonna shoot me?" Matt asked rhetorically, sitting back on the couch like he had no worries. He had no idea that Dave knew everything.

Dave just had to finesse his way of bringing it out because he didn't want Rita to know how he got the information. He wanted to resolve the whole situation before she found out it was his boy that had Shay. Most importantly, he wanted to try to save Shay's life because Lump already had it in his mind that he was going to kill her after he got paid, despite what anybody said.

Dave calmly walked over to the table where Matt's gun was sitting and grabbed it before he had any ideas of being a cowboy. He sat down on the love seat right across from Matt and pointed the .357 Sig at his chest.

"You know, I was driving to my mother's house when I started to think about how foul you are," Dave began. "I watched your body language and ya attitude ever since I walked through that door earlier, and you know what? I saw something in you."

"Yeah, and what's that?" Matt said like he was being entertained by Dave's upcoming analysis.

"For one, if my girl got kidnapped, I wouldn't be sitting in the house looking at fuckin' TV. I would be out on the streets doin' one of two things, and that's either tryin' to find out who got my girl, or racking up some fuckin' money for when somebody call for a ransom. You ain't offer Rita a fuckin' dime of ya money, and you sittin' here like you ain't got nothin' to worry about," Dave said, waving his gun to the rhythm of his words. "Another thing I notice about you is that you do a lot of crying, but not one tear fell from y'all eyes. When I was a kid, I used to do the same thing, right before my mom would whoop my ass so she would feel guilty about what she was doin'. It worked all the way up until my mom figured out I was faking, and then she'd beat the shit out of me. But you, you really don't care what happens to Shay."

"Fuck you, nigga. I love my girl," Matt shot back, sitting up on the edge of the couch.

Rita looked on, doing the math in her head as Dave exposed Matt. He was right about what he was saying, and Rita couldn't deny that. She kinda noticed the same things, but she overlooked it because of who he was. Matt just sat there with a stupid look on his face, doing his best to avoid eye contact with Rita.

"Don't you know dese niggas is going to kill ya girl whether they get the money or not?" Dave continued. "They are going to blow her fuckin' head off, and you're going to let 'em."

"I told you I don't know nothin'," Matt said, becoming sad at the thought of Shay being shot.

"You're lying, and now I'm done fuckin' wit' you. You have a choice to make right now, and your choice is going to determine if you live or die. If you tell me where Shay is, I give you my word that I won't kill you, and if you don't, I'ma blow ya fuckin' brains all over that couch, and that's word on my mother's life," Dave said, taking the safety off of his gun and pointing it at Matt's face. "You got five seconds."

"Rita, get ya boyfriend," Matt said, becoming scared looking down the barrel of Dave's gun.

"Four," Dave announced, staring him in the eyes.

"Dave," Rita said, trying to get his attention.

"Three," he counted, moving the gun closer to Matt's face.

Matt looked up at Rita, hoping that she would be able to stop it, but all she did was turn her head as though she didn't want to see it. He then turned back to look at Dave, who had a stone look on his face, and the sound of him hollering out the number two, sent chills through his body. It's one thing to be shot by somebody, but to be shot in the face and to see it coming was a whole other ball game. Matt just put his head down, seeing his life pass him by.

"One," Dave said. He was just about to pull the trigger, but words coming from Matt's mouth broke the silence in the room.

"She at Isis's dad house," Matt said, picking his head up to look at Rita with a sorrowful look on his face. "They said that they wasn't going to kill her and that all they wanted was the money," Matt said, now starting to cry with real tears.

"So, you was in on dis shit the whole time?" Rita asked, furious as to his disloyalty.

"Yeah, man, I was wit' it. I was wit' it," Matt cried, flopping back on the couch, ashamed of what he had done.

Rita calmly walked over to Dave and grabbed Matt's gun, which was sitting on his lap. She felt nothing inside. No remorse, no guilt, no sympathy, no nothing. Matt had crossed the line into a boundary that was forbidden, and there was no reason why he should enjoy another breath on earth. She raised the gun up to his head and waited for him to look her in the eyes. She wanted to be the last person he saw before his last moments.

"Wait. You gave me ya word you wasn't going to kill me," he yelled out to Dave.

"You're right. I'm not going to," Dave said, lowering his weapon, as to honor his word.

Matt looked up at Rita, whose gun was still pointed at his head. Boom! Matt's head exploded, pulling brain fragment along with it and splattering all over the couch. She didn't stop there, turning the gun on Dave next. She was at the point where she didn't know who she could trust anymore. She wondered how Dave knew that Matt had something to do with Shay's kidnapping. How did he know that the kidnappers were going to kill her sister after they got the money? She thought about the phone call he'd received right before he left the house, and then all of a sudden he came back with a hunch Matt was in on it. It was all bullshit, and Dave better start explaining himself or his head would be taken off as well.

"How did you know?" Rita asked, tears falling down her face and the gun pointed directly at Dave's chest.

Dave had to be careful of what he said and did because Rita was itchy on the trigger, and one false move could cost him his life. He took his finger off the trigger of his gun nice and slow, showing Rita that he wasn't a threat in no way, shape, or form. He placed the gun on the table in front of him and put his hands in the air where Rita could see them.

"Rita, put the gun down," he said, standing to his feet slowly, giving her eye to eye contact the whole time.

"No. Tell me, how did you know?" she screamed out, clutching the gun with both hands nice and tight.

Dave just stood there, showing no signs of fear or worry that Rita was going to shoot him. He remained calm and collected, dropping his hands to his side. He knew that beyond a shadow of a doubt, Rita would have shot him if he sat there and told her that his friends were the ones who had her sister. It was a no-brainer, and even though he wanted to tell her, he couldn't, not here and now, and maybe not ever if he could help it.

"Let me ask you something, Rita. How do you know how to cook and cut up cocaine so good? To know how much bake to add, or when is the right time to add the ice after the oils drop to the bottom of the pot?" Dave asked, calmly taking slow steps toward her. "How do you know to distribute the right amount of product to each corner that you own without giving too much or not giving enough?" he asked, stepping within inches of Rita's gun pointing directly at his chest. "Hell, you do it for so long it becomes second nature to you. You learn from experience until you damn near perfect ya art. Dis shit right here," he said, pointing to Matt's body slumped over the couch, "I been doin' dis shit since I was a kid. I can't explain to you how, but . . . I just know," he told Rita, stepping so close that the gun started pressing against his chest. "If you don't believe me, just pull the trigger."

Rita found it hard to be able to pull the trigger, looking into his eyes and seeing his sincerity. Everything in her gut was telling her to believe him, to trust him, and to feel secure in knowing that Dave would never hurt her. She didn't know what to do. All she knew was that the man she was falling in love with was standing on the other end of her gun.

"You can trust me," Dave said in a soft, calm, and assertive voice, slowly reaching his hand up and moving the gun away from his chest.

"I'm sorry," she cried, leaning in to rest her head upon his chest, tossing the gun onto the couch next to Matt's dead body.

Dave wrapped his arms around her, knowing exactly what she needed. No kissing, like it would have been called for in a movie. No snapping over the fact that she could have shot him. Just a hug. That's what Rita needed at this point. A hug meant more than the average person could understand. It was that sense of security, the sense of understanding, the piece of mind to know that somebody was there for her for a change. This was exactly what she needed.

"You know we gotta get rid of this body," David said with a little humor, looking over at Matt. "And ya couch."

Chapter 18

Shay could hear footsteps upstairs, walking through the house. After a few moments, they stopped right at the basement door. She didn't know how long she'd been in the pitch black basement. With no windows and no light, she lost track of time. Shay couldn't see anything, not even if her own hand was in front of her face. She couldn't understand why she was put in the basement in the first place, seeing as how she wasn't causing any problems upstairs.

It wasn't long before the door opened and the light came on, causing Shay to squint. It took a couple of moments for her eyes to adjust to the light, but when they did, taking a seat on the steps was Isis. Shay didn't know what she came down there for, but the look on Isis's face showed that it was a friendly visit. No fighting, no cursing one another, just a regular conversation was all Isis was looking for.

"I don't have anything to say to you, so you might as well take ya ass back upstairs," Shay said, not even looking in Isis's direction.

"Come on, li'l cousin. You think I wanted all this?" Isis shot back, beginning to feel just a little remorse for how far things had escalated. Her face being all over the news for murder had made her realize that none of what she did was worth what she had coming if she ever got caught.

She didn't even realize that the police were the least of her worries. It was Rita who she had to worry about, because no matter what she said or how sorry she was, Rita was going to stop at nothing in her quest to kill Isis. That was etched in stone, and Isis might have been better off turning herself in if she only knew.

A toy flying down the steps caught Isis's attention. Turning around to see the little girl standing at the top of the steps, she quickly ran upstairs to grab her before the little girl fell. Isis brought the cute, fat-faced little girl down the steps, making her say hi.

Shay looked up at the little girl and could see somewhat of a resemblance between the two.

"Whose kid you got down here?" Shay asked, curious as to who would let their child be around all this drama.

"Oh, this little angel? This little angel is my daughter. Her name is Briana, and she just turned two last month," Isis said, smiling as she tickled the little girl.

"Daughter?" Shay asked in shock.

"Yeah. Remember when I got locked up a few years back for the drugs and guns they found in my car?" she explained. "The whole year that I was locked up, I was pregnant for nine of those months. Nobody but my dad knew about her. Not even her dad."

"Who is her dad?" Shay asked out of curiosity.

"I really didn't want anybody to know about her. I didn't want her to grow up like we did," Isis continued, avoiding Shay's last question. "As I look back and think about it, I guess you can say she's the reason why I got this scar running down the side of my face. And for the record, I never stole any money from your sister. I was probably more loyal to her than anybody."

In a way, Isis wanted to tell Shay that she was sorry for everything that had happened, but it was far too late for apologies. People died, money was wasted, and lives were ruined. An apology wouldn't mean nothin' but a smack in the face. Besides, Shay wasn't buying all the sob stories Isis was tellin', and the only reason she sat there listening to her was because she really didn't have a choice.

There was one thing that picked at her brain, though, and she couldn't help but to repeat her previous question again, now seeing another familiar resemblance in the little girl's face. "You never answered my question," Shay said, looking up at Isis, knowing she had heard her the first time.

Isis hesitated, looking at Briana sitting in her lap. At this point, it didn't even matter how anybody felt about her. One of three things was going happen. Isis would go to prison for the rest of her life, die in a blaze of glory, or get this money and move away to a quiet town where nobody knew her.

"Matt is her dad," Isis said. Before Shay could respond to her comment, she shot back up the step, turned the lights out, and closed the door, once again leaving Shay in the dark.

Dave and Rita drove down 1-95 on their way to Isis's dad's house in Newcastle, Delaware. Dave was doing the speed limit the entire way. Rita was impatient and kept telling Dave to hurry up.

"You forget, we've got guns on the car. We don't need to get pulled over and taken to jail. Then you'll never see Shay again."

"I'm gonna fuck Isis up," Rita said.

"Look, we goin' there to get a better picture of what's going on. We ain't going in guns blazing."

"You right. But I'm still gonna fuck that bitch up."

Dave laughed. "Okay, but our first priority, we gotta get rid of the body in the trunk," Dave said, referring to Matt's body.

Isis's dad lived in Oakmont, just after Wilmington. Rita was somewhat familiar with Delaware, because her father used to take her out there when she was younger. She'd remembered a park they used to go to for cookouts and reunions, and she thought that it would be the perfect spot to dump Matt off. As they drove through the park, they searched for a place where there were no people, and although the occasional jogger ran through these parts, Rita thought of a spot right by a creek, about a quarter of a mile inside a wooded area, away from the public eye.

She pulled into the area as far as the road would let her, and parked. "We got to carry him the rest of the way," she told Dave, looking around to see if anybody was watching.

Dave couldn't get this stupid smirk off his face. He was taken away by the fact that he was able to witness Rita putting in some work, something he never saw a woman doing, especially one that he was seeing. *She is gangsta,* he thought to himself, watching her pop the trunk as though this was something she had done before, grabbing a hold of Matt's feet, showing her willingness to help carry him. Dave's smirk turned into a smile at the sight of that.

"Move, girl," he chuckled, looking around one last time before pulling Matt's body out of the trunk and tossing him over his shoulder.

Rita walked behind Dave as he headed into the woods, all the while looking around to make sure the coast was clear. The blood from Matt's head leaked into the trash bag that was tied around his head, and when they got to the edge of the creek, Dave took Matt's clothes off to avoid any forensic evidence that could possibly be traced back to him or Rita.

Rita stood over Matt, kicking his body down the short hill which led to the stream. The sounds of her phone ringing took her attention off of watching him float away. It was at that point she realized that it was far past two o'clock, and most likely she had missed the kidnappers' call.

"Who dis?" she answered, walking back to the car next to Dave.

"I want two million for ya sista. You pay the tab, I'll let her go. If you don't, I'll kill her, then come after you next," the voice on the end of the phone demanded. "I'll call back at six o'clock to let you know where to take the money."

"How do I know she's still alive? Let me talk to her," Rita asked, only wanting to confirm that Shay was still alive.

"Bitch, dis ain't the movies. Get the money, have it ready, and answer the phone at six," the voice said then hung up.

Rita didn't even have to tell Dave who was on the phone. He was well aware that Lump was going to try to negotiate a deal without him. That's the reason why Dave turned off his phone. If Lump couldn't reach him, he was going to do exactly what Dave predicted he was going to do. He knew Lump better than anybody, and he was using what Lump lacked, to work in his favor: patience. Lump didn't have a lick of it, and that was the reason why he was calling Rita's phone. Everything was coming along just the way Dave figured it would.

"How much do they want?" Dave asked, getting back into the car.

"They want two million by six o'clock. I don't even have two million. I got like one point five million in cash right now and about twenty bricks of cocaine left. It's no way I'ma come up wit' dat kind of money by six, two hours away."

Dave was shocked to even hear that she had that much money on hand. Lump was right about Rita having cake. He was even more shocked that Lump would ask for that kind of money in such short notice.

That wasn't a bad price to negotiate, he thought to himself, somewhat impressed with Lump's growth. He was starting off good, but it never matters the way you start. It only counts how you finish, and in that aspect, Dave was the better man.

"Change of plans. Go back to the city," Dave instructed Rita, pulling out his cell phone and turning it back on.

"Why? What's going on?" she asked with a concerned look on her face.

"Dis the last time I'ma ask you to trust me," Dave said with a smile on his face, quickly punching in some numbers on his phone. "I'ma hold you down. Just ride wit' me on this one."

"Detective Mozar," another detective announced, coming into his office holding a folder in her hand. "An anonymous call just came in, and they wanted to speak to the detective in charge of the Chanel Thompkins case. I have her on my line," she said, still standing at his door.

"Patch her through to my line," he told the detective, staring up at the wall of evidence he had on Isis.

Up until now, every anonymous tip pretty much led to a dead end, so the excitement of hearing about another one didn't quite reach Mozar. He'd been sitting in his office all afternoon, trying to figure out where in the world could Isis be. He had searched every residence she ever lived in, including her grandmother's house, and still nothing. He even searched two houses that were given to him from an anonymous tip, but still nothing. This was the part of the job where he became frustrated, just about giving up and moving to the next case. For all he knew, Isis was out of the city by now.

He looked over at his phone as it began to ring. He closed his eyes and took a deep breath, hoping this call would give him a strong lead.

"Detective Mozar," he answered, exhaling the deep breath he took before answering the phone.

"I got information on Chanel Thompkins," a deep, manly voice said on the other end. "I know exactly where she's at right this second, and trust me, it's not a game."

"Okay, I hear you, buddy. Just let me know where she's at so you can claim the reward," Mozar said, tempting the caller with money.

"Look, the only way I'ma tell you where she's at is if you come get her yourself. I'll let you bring one other cop car wit' you, but that's it. I got kids in my house, and I don't want to scare them."

"Yeah, yeah, I can make that happen, but there's some things I need to know before I put myself or your children in harm's way," Mozar said, concerned about Isis having a gun.

This phone call was a lot different from the rest of the phone calls he'd received. This one actually sounded promising. Mozar was excited all over again, just like a kid in a candy store. He didn't mind the fact that he could only bring one other cop car with him. He actually preferred that, wanting to take all of the credit for the biggest arrest in the city.

Chapter 19

Rita stopped at her grandmother's house to grab the $1.5 million she kept there. It was for this current situation why she didn't keep that kind of money at her own house. Of course, Ms. Scott had a million and one questions for Rita, including her curiosity about the cute young man she had with her. Rita got in and out of her grandmother's house within minutes, knowing that she didn't have much time until the kidnappers called back.

It only took twenty minutes for Rita to get from her grandmother's house to Dave's mother's house, where he kept the bulk of his money. Rita was surprised by how close it was to her own house. She assumed she'd probably seen Dave's mother around the neighborhood before. She was kind of surprised she'd never seen Dave before.

"Why didn't you tell me your mom lived in my neighborhood?"

"I didn't think of it. I was too focused on your phat ass."

Rita punched Dave in his shoulder. "Stop being fresh." She smiled.

She pulled into the driveway, and the older lady, who was watching her flowers, popped her head up to see the unfamiliar car.

"Do you see that lady right there?" Dave pointed while Rita turned off the car. "That's my moms."

Rita was somewhat speechless. She didn't know what to say. This was her first time meeting his mother, and given the circumstances, this probably wasn't a good time. First impressions were the best impression, so if moms didn't approve of the newfound relationship, it was pretty much a wrap. It scared Rita so much that she didn't even want to get out of the car, but a tap on the window and Ms. Betty standing there motioning for her to get out of the car changed her mind.

"Get ya ass out dat car! My son been talking about you for the past week."

You couldn't blame Ms. Betty for not knowing what was going on. She was only being herself, still a little hood. She grew up in North Philly and raised Dave all by herself. It wasn't but a few years ago that he moved her out of Montgomery County, Pennsylvania, to get away from all the crime in the city.

It was shocking that Dave would show up unannounced and with a young lady with him, but Ms. Betty was always prepared. They could still smell the fried chicken coming from the house, and that alone reminded Rita of how hungry she was, considering she hadn't eaten all day.

She pulled Rita out of the car and stood directly in front of her for a motherly inspection. Dave quickly made his way into the house to grab his money and hopefully leave before his mother wanted something. She sized Rita up first, looking at her from head to toe, checking out the way she dressed.

Rita tried to introduce herself, but Ms. Betty shushed her and told her not to say a word until she was done. If Rita didn't check out, she wouldn't have to worry about saying hi. Ms. Betty had no shame in dismissing a woman who wasn't good enough for her son.

Before she could even start her inspection, Dave was back out the door, right in time to see the show. He thought about stopping it, but he knew that it would only start a fight, plus he was interested in seeing if his mother approved of Rita. She never approved of any of the fast girls Dave was with. This process never took Ms. Betty long at all.

First, Ms. Betty grabbed a handful of Rita's hair and lightly yanked on it to see if it was real. Rita squirmed a little but stood there smiling at what Dave's mother was doing. Next, she cupped her hands underneath Rita's breasts and bounced them twice, and Rita almost busted out laughing, but she stood her ground, willing to comply with the inspection. Ms. Betty grabbed Rita's hands, lifted them in the air, and twirled her around so that she could see her from the back.

"Her ass is okay, but we can work wit' dat," she said and slapped Rita's backside. "Y'all two go on in the house. I'll be there in a minute."

"Mom, we can't stay," Dave said, trying to give her a kiss before he made his way to the car.

"Hush ya mouth, boy," Ms. Betty snapped back. "Now, sweetie, would you mind coming inside for a quick bite to eat? You sure look hungry to me," Ms. Betty asked Rita in the calmest voice.

At first Rita was hesitant, thinking about what time it was, but there was something about Ms. Betty that brought a sense of tranquility to her, the same way Dave did. She looked at her watch, and it had just turned 5:00. She had a whole hour before the kidnapper called. There really wasn't anything else to do until they called anyway, plus Ms. Betty was right about Rita being hungry.

Without taking no for an answer, Ms. Betty wrapped her arm around Rita and walked her into the house. Dave looked at his watch, too, checking the time before he followed them into the house.

"Rita, I need to talk to you," Dave said, grabbing her arm and walking her into the kitchen.

"Good, because I have something I want to talk to you about too."

There were words they had wanted to say to each other for a while now outside of the current situation. The right time never presented itself, so they were stuck with the feelings they had for each other until the time was right.

They both stood there for a moment in silence, trying to see who was going to go first, but before either of them could say another word, Ms. Betty walked into the kitchen, changing the whole mood. The food was ready, and so was Ms. Betty for round two with Rita. She had to know what was so special about Rita that Dave had brought her to see his mother.

Hell, Rita was still trying to figure out how she had made it this far.

When Ms. Betty served the food, Rita wasted no time getting busy. She maintained her table manners, but the food didn't stand a chance. She didn't come up for air until half of the plate was gone, and Ms. Betty packed on the food. Ms. Betty looked at Dave and cracked a smile.

"Damn, nigga, is you feeding her?" Ms. Betty joked, giggling at the sight of Rita chowing down on her food.

Rita and Dave couldn't help but to chuckle at Ms. Betty's joke. Aside from Rita being hungry, Ms. Betty sure knew how to cook, especially when it came down to fish. Rita ended up finishing her plate before everybody, and when her phone began to ring, the whole room became quiet.

Rita looked at Dave, then Ms. Betty. "Excuse me. I really need to take this." She walked all the way outside and stood on the front porch.

Dave watched her pass back and forth in front of the window, and just as fast as she went outside, she came back in.

"I'm so sorry. That was my sister. She has an emergency I need to help her with."

"Oh, honey. Don't apologize. Family comes first, always." Ms. Betty smiled.

Dave thought it was time to go. He looked at Rita, but Rita shook her head no and motioned with her hand for Dave to pump his brakes.

"Family is so important to me. After my mother died, it was just me and my sister. I'm so lucky I had a sister to lean on in those difficult times. I don't know what I would have done without her. We grew up in West Philadelphia, not the most pleasant neighborhood for two orphaned girls. The streets were ruthless, but we had each other's backs. She saved me many times, and I saved her."

"You're lucky to have her. I'd love to meet her someday," Ms. Betty said. "I feel the same way about my family. The day I met David's father, I knew he was the only family I was ever going to need. I grew up in a single parent home. My mother loved me and did everything she could to give me a better life than she had. She worked three jobs and then paid my way through college. I can't believe I went to college, let alone received my master's degree in math.

"Math didn't come easy to me at first, but my mother would sit at the kitchen table with me and help me through all my math worksheets. She had the patience of a saint. Eventually, I saw the beauty in numbers and fell in love with math. Now I want to give David here a better life than I had. I would do anything for him." She looked straight at Rita. "Even put a bullet in someone if they ever hurt my David."

But at the end of the night, Ms. Betty gave Dave a nod, letting him know that she approved of Rita. That alone was big, and it just made things easier for him.

"Now, I been up wit' y'all all evening, and it's almost time for me to go to bed. David, you lock that door behind you and turn off all the lights down here," Ms. Betty said before getting up from the dining room table. "You bring this pretty girl back over here to see me." She leaned over to kiss Rita on the forehead, which shocked the hell out of Dave.

Finally, with Ms. Betty upstairs, Rita and Dave were all alone. They had wanted to talk for the past two hours and oftentimes made eye contact with each other while Ms. Betty was talking.

Dave was curious as to the nature of the phone call, seeing as how it was already going on seven o'clock and Rita hadn't moved out of her seat. She even looked like she was enjoying the conversation she was having with Ms. Betty.

"So what happened?" Dave asked, checking the status of the situation.

"They want me to bring the money to the plateau out Fairmount Park at nine. They told me to come by myself."

Her going out to Fairmount Park by herself was definitely out of the question. Dave knew exactly what that meant. Lump was going to leave Rita there stinking as soon as he got the money, and it would only be a matter of time before he went back and killed Shay. Dave had to think. He wanted to be able to see that everybody made out. He didn't want to have to choose between Rita and his boys, and it got to the point where he wanted to tell Rita everything.

"I need to tell you something, but I don't want you to get mad," Dave began. "Before I met you . . . well, since I met you . . . I really don't know how to say this."

Dave could hardly get the words out that he wanted to say. He started thinking about the connection he had with her and how happy she'd made him in the past two weeks. He thought about dinner tonight, and how well she bonded with his mom. He thought about how good it felt to wake up next to her in the morning, and how incredible the sex was. He thought about the possibility of having a future with her, and maybe even putting the ring she had on her finger to good use. Then, he thought about seeing her body lying in a coffin, stiff and pale.

"Do you believe in love at first sight?" Rita asked him, cutting off his mumbling.

It caught him by surprise. "What?" he asked just to make sure that he heard her right.

Rita was kind of embarrassed to have asked it the first time, so to ask it again was killing her. "I said, do you believe in love at first sight?" This time she scooted her chair close to him so that she could grab his hand.

"Well, that depends on what ya definition for love is. For me, love is when you no longer live for yourself. From the time you wake up until the time you go to bed at night, you sacrifice ya freedom, ya happiness, ya wealth, ya time, ya knowledge, and all other worldly things in order to share them with someone else. A lot of people take love for granted, and they never take the time out to truly understand what the word means. The moment I laid my eyes on you, you had a smile on ya face, and I thought to myself that I would do anything to keep that smile on ya face, even if I had to sacrifice my life. So, to answer your question correctly, I don't believe in love at first sight. I believe in preordained love, meaning that only God knew exactly how I would feel about you when He did it."

Rita was speechless. This was probably the reason why she felt the way that she did. It was like what Dave had said. He was reading her mind. She was scared to say it. She wanted to say it, but she didn't want to look like a fool or feel dumb in the event that he didn't feel the same way, but it was official. Rita fell in love with a man that she barely knew.

"I wanted to ask you something. I told you I was going to hold you down and help with the ransom, and alto-gcthcr I have seven hundred K to my name. I'ma give you five hundred of that, and I was thinking maybe . . ."

"What?" she said, hearing him pause. "What was you thinking?"

"I was thinking maybe me and you could take the rest of the money and roll out. You know, move far away and start our lives over again. We can bring Shay wit' us if you want." He smiled. "I just think we both could use a fresh start."

The idea was pretty much everything Rita had in mind anyway. It was time to let go of the street life. Shay sitting in a basement with a two-million-dollar ransom was a strong reminder of how a change in her life was necessary. Here, she had a good man standing in front of her, offering the chance to live a normal life, which meant him giving up his old way of life. He'd been good to Rita, and the bond that they had built from meeting in a jewelry store to dumping bodies in creeks was stronger than anything.

"Dave, I think I'm—"

"David, are you still down there?" Ms. Betty yelled from upstairs, cutting Rita off before she could say another word.

"Yeah, Mom, I'm on my way out the door right now. I'll give you a call tomorrow," he yelled back, standing up to leave.

"Bye, Ms. Betty. It was a pleasure to meet you," Rita yelled upstairs, also standing to her feet.

"Bye, baby. You come back over here anytime you want. You're always welcome in my home."

It got dark while they were in the house, but the night was beautiful. The stars were out, the moon split in half, and the air smelled fresh. Dave stopped and leaned up against the car, wrapping Rita up in his arms.

"Everything is going to be okay, I promise you," Dave said, ensuring Rita of her sister's safe return.

He leaned in to kiss her, but from out of his peripheral, he could see a car that looked way too familiar. It was Lump's car, sitting directly across the street. Dave looked into the sky and took in a deep breath, knowing that it was about to be some bullshit. The Glock 9 mm tucked in his back waistband gave him a little feeling of security in the event things escalated to gunplay.

It was like Lump and Cees came out of nowhere, walking up the driveway with guns in their hands, and by the time Dave started to lean off of the car, they were already standing about ten feet away.

Rita thought they were about to get robbed, and the first thing she started to do was reach into her pocketbook for her gun. Dave quickly stopped her, knowing that if she had pulled out that gun, Lump was going to start shooting without hesitation.

"Something told me that you was getting soft on me," Lump said, clutching the gun tightly in his hand. "I said to myself, *'Self, follow him and see what he's up to.'*"

"C'mon, dog. It is what it is," Dave said, leaning off of the car so that he was facing him.

"It is what it is!" Lump said sarcastically. "So, what is it? You savin' dis bitch?"

"Bitch! Who da fuck you think you callin' a bitch?" Rita snapped back. "What the hell is going on, Dave?"

"Yeah, Dave, tell her what's going on, bro. Tell her how we planned on robbing her, then blowing her fuckin' top off."

"*What?* You were going to kill me?" she asked with hurt in her eyes.

Dave snatched Rita up by her arms, trying to get her attention. "Look at me! Look at me, Rita!" he yelled, seeing that she was about to cry. "I swear, I didn't even know who you were. He didn't even tell me that it was you until a couple of hours ago, and I didn't want to tell you because I wasn't going to let dis shit go down. Look at me . . . look at me!" he said, seeing her looking over his shoulder at Cees.

"Do you remember what I told you in the house about what love is? It's the truth, and I'm standing here right now willing to sacrifice everything for you."

Hearing Dave talk like that only made Lump angrier. He and Dave were best friends, and nobody had ever come in between them, not even the bullet Lump took for Dave a couple of years ago over something Dave did. They were homies for life, and that's what they had agreed on since they were kids. This shit was starting to get bigger than Rita.

"So, you gonna choose dis bitch over me, my nigga?" Lump asked, raising his gun and pointing it at Rita. "Nigga, I raised you! All the shit I did for you, and you're gonna play me like dis! Where da fuck is the loyalty?" he yelled under his clenched teeth.

"I am loyal," Dave said, grabbing Rita and putting her behind him. "You might want to explain to Cees how loyal you been, fucking Ashley."

That was the straw that broke the camel's back for Lump. He pointed the gun at Dave, closed his eyes, and squeezed the trigger. The bullet ripped into Dave's chest and knocked him backward into Rita. She caught him, and at the same time they were falling to the ground, Rita pulled the Glock from Dave's back, reached around, and started firing in Lump's direction.

She counted every bullet that left her gun, *One, two, three, four, five, six, seven,* all of them hitting Lump from the waist up. When she got to number eight, she turned the gun on Cees, who took off running around the car. Rita fired, chasing him down with bullet after bullet.

You could hear the bullets hitting the car and breaking every window. Cees ran fast until Rita emptied the whole clip.

She reach for her pocketbook to grab her gun, just in case Cees didn't go that far, but by the time she got her hand on the gun, she felt a piece of steel pressing up against the back of her head. Cees had run around the car only to run up from behind Rita. She knew for sure that this was it. She braced herself for impact, releasing the gun in her pocketbook and wrapping her arms around Dave. If she was goin' to die, this was how she wanted to go.

"For what it's worth, Dave didn't know we was going to rob you, and the only reason why I'm not squeezing this trigger is on the strength of Dave and the respect I got for your sister," Cees said, lowering the gun from Rita's head and backing up slowly.

Rita let out a sigh of relief, glad that Cees didn't kill her.

Dave lay on the ground, choking on his own blood and gasping for air. His body was going into shock, and although Rita put pressure to his chest to stop the bleeding, she could see signs of life leaving him.

"Please don't die, baby! Hold on! I'm right here!" she cried out. "Please don't leave me! Come on, baby. Fight! *Somebody help me-e-e-e-e!*" she screamed at the top of her lungs. She looked down at Dave. His eye were drowsy like he was high off something, and he kept going in and out of consciousness.

The tears rushed down her face. "I love you, David! Do you hear me? I love you, boy! Please don't leave me!" she cried out. "*Somebody help me-e-e-e-e!*"

Chapter 20

The hospital waiting room was packed with homicide detectives, asking Rita every question they could think of. She stuck to a basic story, saying that she and Dave were being robbed and that she shot the perpetrator after he shot Dave. When asked about the gun she used to shoot him with, she claimed it, saying that the gun was hers, even though it wasn't registered in her name. She did, however, produce a license to carry, and since the gun wasn't reported stolen, the most she could get was a citation for not having a registered gun. Of course, detectives took the gun because a murder was committed with it.

Ms. Betty stood outside of the room as doctors worked on Dave. The bullet ripped through his chest and caused a lot of damage on its way out through his upper back. If the bullet had hit him three inches below, it would have hit him directly in his heart, killing him instantly.

Hell, if Rita was a little bit taller and her head was slightly to the left, she wouldn't be sitting in the waiting room right now. She'd be in the morgue.

After extensive questioning, Rita walked into the emergency room and joined Ms. Betty outside of Dave's room. The sight of all the blood and doctors sticking tubes here and tubes there made Rita cry. She'd seen people die, saw people shot, even on the other end of her gun, but this was the first time she witnessed somebody actually fighting for their life. That's exactly what Dave was doing, fighting. He had already flatlined once, and there had to be at least three doctors and three nurses working on him at the same time.

It took every bit of three hours just to get him stabilized. A doctor came out to the waiting room with that specific piece of news, but he was not sure whether he was going to make it through the night. The bullet did so much damage the doctor didn't think his body was capable of recovering from it, and if he did make it through the night, there was no telling when he would wake up out of his coma. The news was devastating, and it was almost like Dave had already died. Furthermore, Rita still had another problem she had to deal with, and without further delay, she got up and walked out of the waiting room with a firm, fixed, focused look on her face. She didn't even say goodbye to Ms. Betty, who just watched as Rita stormed out of the hospital.

It was just a little after midnight, when Rita left the hospital, and once in the parking lot, she noticed a body leaning up against her car from a distance. She didn't know who it was, and frankly, she didn't care. As she got close enough to see who it was, her heart began to race. If there was anything in the world she wanted right now, it was a gun. Her bravery allowed her to walk right up on him, that and the fact he was leaning on the driver-side door of her car.

"How is he?" Cees asked, concerned about the well-being of his best friend.

Lump's actions pretty much took everybody by surprise. Shooting Dave was the last thing Cees thought Lump would do. They were all best friends, and throughout the years of growing up, there was nothing that could ever make them turn on one another, especially money or women. He actually started to feel bad for Rita and Shay, and even worse for Dave. When he actually got a chance to think about everything, none of it was really worth it.

"He's not doing good at all," she answered with a sorrowful look on her face like she was ready to break down and cry again.

"So, I guess you're going to get ya sista," he said, pulling a gun from his back pocket.

Rita just stood there and didn't say a word. At this point, she wasn't even worried about him pulling the trigger, thinking to herself about the possibility of Shay being dead by now. Rita took another step closer, fearlessly. Cees could see the same spunk Rita had in her eyes as did Shay when Lump called himself trying to beat the information out of her. Rita had heart, and to see this coming from a woman, Cees had no other choice but to respect it.

"Ya sista is still alive. She's tied up in the basement for now. In exactly one hour, I'ma call Isis and tell her to come outside and get her cut of the money. That should be more than enough time and opportunity to do what you need to do," Cees said, passing Rita the .40 cal he pulled out.

Rita grabbed the gun and was tempted to blow Cees' head off, but she gave him a pass considering the fact that he had spared her life before. She just brushed by him and got into her car, focusing back on her mission at hand. She sped out of the parking lot at high speed, racing for the expressway as though she were in the Indy 500.

Cees also jumped in his car and sped out, racing in the opposite direction for different reasons. He had a little unfinished business to take care of as well.

Mozar, his partner, and the two other officers he was allowed to bring, lined up next to the house the anonymous caller told him Isis would be at. The officers spread out. Mozar took the front door, his partner took the back, and the other cops stood on the side of the house. Mozar walked onto the front porch and heard the sound of a little girl laughing. A glimpse through the window revealed a woman's back, walking into the kitchen. On the table in front of the couch, in plain view, it looked like a large revolver sitting there, which intensified everything.

Mozar didn't want to give Isis a chance to come back in the room and gain access to the gun, so he just reacted. He took a step back and kicked the front door as hard as he could, somewhat cracking it open. The loud noise got the attention of the woman, who ran out of the kitchen. Mozar's heart began to race even faster thinking she was headed for the gun. He kicked the door again and again until it finally popped open. He ran into the house with his gun drawn, stopping the woman in her tracks.

"Down on the ground! Get down on the ground!" Mozar screamed out, almost shooting her where she stood.

Surprisingly, the woman didn't look anything like Isis, nor was there anybody else in the house when the other officers swarmed and searched it from top to bottom. Mozar not only felt disappointed again, but this time, it was mixed with a little embarrassment. He bragged to his partner the whole way there about how he was going to get promoted from this bust and how he was going to be the one on the news bringing her in. The only thing that he had done tonight was scare the hell out of an innocent woman and her daughter. To add insult to injury, the gun on the table wasn't even real. It was her son's toy. He had left it there before he went to bed an hour ago.

Cees parked four blocks away and walked the rest of the way home. He had a lot of time to think on his way there about Ashley and Lump and how foul both of them were if what Dave said was true. Rita had killed Lump before Cees could even inquire about it or before Lump could get a chance to state his case. It was kind of starting to add up in Cees' mind of how Ashley used to act when Lump used to come around and how friendly she was with him. Then he thought about the day that he followed her and she stopped a couple of blocks from where he had a house in Germantown. All he wanted to do at this point was hear it from the horse's mouth.

It hurt him to even think that his best friend and his wife would betray him like that, and as he turned his key in the door and walked in the house, that hurt quickly turned to anger. The house was quiet. Seeing as how it was one o'clock in the morning, Ashley was upstairs in the bed, asleep with the baby.

He went straight to the kitchen and grabbed the .38 snub from out of the cabinet where he kept it in case of emergency. Walking up the steps, flashes of Lump fucking Ashley from the back went through his mind, and the sounds of her screaming out his name echoed through his ears. It seemed like he would never make it upstairs with all the stopping and pausing he did.

He finally made it to the bedroom, where Ashley was sound asleep with the baby lying right next to her. The light from the TV shone through the room, and as he stood over Ashley, Cees pressed the gun up against her side, nudging her so that she would wake up. It took a few times, but Ashley eventually woke up, startled by the presence of Cees standing over her with a gun in his hand.

"What's going on, boo?" Ashley said, trying to adjust her eyes to the dark room.

"Look, I'ma ask you a couple questions, and I honestly want to know the truth," Cees said in the calmest voice Ashley ever heard from him.

Ashley thought to herself that Cees was going to ask her about something concerning the situation with her cheating on him, and when he sat down on the bed next to her, she immediately sat up, seeing the hurt in his eyes. He took in a deep breath, then scratched his head with the gun, contemplating whether he should continue down this road not knowing how he was going to react to Ashley's answers to his questions.

"Why was you in Germantown a couple of day ago?" was the first question Cees shot out there.

"What are you talking about Germantown for?" she answered with a curious look on her face.

"I followed you that day you said you was going out wit' Keisha. I followed you up Wayne Ave. and watched you park, and then after a while, you pulled off and headed back home. So again, I'ma ask you, why was you in Germantown? And please, don't lie to me and say that it wasn't you."

Ashley didn't know what to say. She wanted to tell him the truth, but she knew it would kill Cees to know that she slept with his best friend. At the same time, she didn't want to sit here and continue to lie in his face, especially since he probably already knew the answers to the questions he was asking. She just sat there, confused about what to do, and the dumb look she had on her face was almost a confession in itself.

Cees quickly got tired of beating around the bush, seeing that it wasn't getting him anywhere. He just came right out wit' it. No cut cards, no bullshit attached to it. One question, and only one answer he expected in return.

"Did you fuck Lump?" he asked, looking Ashley in her eyes, giving her the feeling that he already knew.

Tears quickly filled Ashley's eyes, and by that action alone, it confirmed what Cees hoped she would deny. It sent a sharp pain through his chest, and his eyes also began to fill up with tears. The betrayal, the disloyalty.

"I'm sorry," Ashley cried out, trying to grab a hold of Cees, who pushed her hands away from him. "I'm sorry, boo. Please forgive me."

Everything from that point on went blank. Cees leaned over and grabbed one of the pillows at the top of the bed. He stuffed the gun in it, pointed it at Ashley, and squeezed the trigger. The muffled sound was followed by a bullet striking Ashley in her lower abdomen. She grabbed her stomach, feeling the hot ball inside of her, and fell over onto the bed. She couldn't even scream because blood started to fill up in her lungs.

Cees stood up off of the bed, pointed the gun at her head, and fired again, this time hitting her right in between the eyes. The sound from the second shot wasn't muffled as well as the first one, so it woke up the baby.

Cees was well prepared for the aftermath of killing Ashley. He went straight to work, cleaning up the mess, opening drawers, throwing a few twenty-dollar bills on the bed and sprinkling some cocaine on the floor, making it look like a home invasion gone bad. He even duct-taped her mouth, hands, and feet together, all while feeding his son and putting him back to sleep before leaving back out the door. The bad part about it was that he felt no remorse for killing Ashley. The pain that she caused outweighed that by a long shot.

Chapter 21

Mozar was hot. He knew for sure that Isis was going to be there, but it turned out to be another dead-end lead. The night wasn't over, though, and in fact, it had just begun. He ditched the two cops that were with him, and he, along with his partner, Seal, headed down Belmont Avenue toward West Philly. He was going to take Rita up on her offer, and during the ride he brought Seal on board with what was going on. There wasn't a question whether Seal was with it. He was just as crooked, if not worse than Mozar, when it came to being a dirty cop.

They got to the area where Rita had sent them and parked two blocks away in order to get ready. They had busted stash houses before, so this one was no different than the rest of them, except that all the evidence would be going home with them instead of the police station. They sat outside of the car, strapping their vests and putting on their police jackets. It even looked like a routine bust.

Once at the house, they went around back. Rita had advised them that the back door was the weakest and would be easier to kick down by one man. They hopped over the fence as quickly as possible, hearing that the dogs in the alley were starting to bark. There was no time to waste at this point. Somebody might get alarmed by the dogs and ruin the whole element of surprise.

"One, two, three," Mozar counted before taking a step back and kicking the back door as hard as he could.

The door came right off the hinges, and in went the two officers, directly into the line of fire. The occupant of the house didn't care that it was the police. He only had one job, and that job was to protect the money and drugs by all costs from whoever walked through that door trying to take it. Bullets were flying from the living room into the kitchen, where Mozar and Seal were, taking cover behind the refrigerator and the floor-model deep freezer. It sounded as though the man had some type of machine gun the way he rapidly fired into the kitchen.

Mozar waved at Seal to get his attention. He raised his fist in the air, motioning for tactical approach they used in real live situations. Seal knew exactly what to do, listening for the gun firing to either slow down or stop completely. It wasn't stopping, though. Seal had to make it stop.

He reached around the refrigerator and fired a few shots into the living room. While he did that, Mozar peeked from behind the deep freezer to see where the shooter was at. He had taken cover behind the entertainment system.

Then, the shooting ceased from the living room. That's when Mozar jumped up from behind the freezer, hoping to catch the shooter before he got a chance to reload his weapon.

"Get ya hands where I can see them," Mozar yelled with his gun pointed at the entertainment system. He moved in closer, listening carefully to any noise that sounded like the reloading of a gun. He wanted, or rather needed, this guy alive for the most part. One false move and Mozar was going to empty his clip into the entertainment system without hesitation.

Mozar got right up on the entertainment system and finally got a visual. The shooter was lying on the ground, holding his stomach. Seal had actually managed to hit him with a lucky shot.

"Seal, you lucky sum'bitch, you hit him," Mozar laughed, standing over the gunman. "From the looks of that wound, you're gonna need some medical attention," he told the shooter, who was conscious but in severe pain.

"Please don't let me die," he pleaded, leaning up against the wall.

"Well, that all is going to depend on you. Now, I know there's money and drugs in here, so don't lie to me," Mozar said, kneeling down next to him.

"I don't know what you're talking about."

"I guess you're going to lay here and die slow, and while you're busy doing that, I'll be tearing this house apart piece by piece until I find it."

Mozar was serious. He'd come too far to leave that house empty handed. He also didn't have that much time before the real police showed up, and he'd have to give an excuse as to why he was making a drug bust in a totally different district than he was assigned to.

"Hold up, man. Call an ambulance and I'll tell you where the money is. I don't want to die," the man pleaded.

"First you tell me where it's at, and then I'll get you to the hospital," Mozar lied.

The man looked over at the 40-inch flat screen TV sitting on the wall above the mantle and pointed to it. Seal immediately walked over to it and pushed it off the brackets it hung on, throwing it to the ground. Behind it was a small door dug inside of the wall. Seal grabbed a chair stood on it and pulled the latch. Inside was a safe, about twenty inches long and wide, and the size of it looked like it could fit more than 50k in it.

"What's the combination?" Seal yelled out.

The gunman spit it out as quickly as he could, wanting nothing else but to get some medical attention. Once the safe door opened, Seal almost fell off the chair looking inside. There was way more than 50k there, and that was just on the lower shelf. The top shelf was stacked with a number of bricks of cocaine. Seal cracked a smile, looking over at Mozar, who was still kneeling over the gunman.

"Jackpot!" he declared, pulling a stack of money out of the safe and tossing it to his partner. "We hit the gotdamn jackpot."

Chapter 22

Rita pulled into the Oakmont development where Isis's dad lived. She had almost forgotten her way around but quickly remembered the area after driving down a couple streets. This neighborhood was somewhat ghetto but more on the upscale side, so it wasn't surprising that a couple of people were still outside after 1:00 in the morning.

She stopped on the top of the block the house was on and parked. Rita headed straight for her trunk, knowing that Cees would be calling Isis any minute now. The first thing that she grabbed was the bulletproof vest, strapping it on and stuffing the .40 cal under it.

Two dudes sat across the street on an abandoned porch, watching as Rita geared up, and instead of drawing any attention to her, they sat back and waited to see what was going to happen next.

When Rita pulled "the Last Airbender" out of her trunk, it damn near stood as tall as her. The sight of that big-ass gun in her hands shocked the two dudes sitting on the porch, and for a hot second, one of them said a quick prayer asking God for it not to be them she was coming to see.

Rita walked past them and headed down the street for Isis's house. She waited on the opposite side of the street, directly across from the house, with the gun mounted on top of a parked car. She just sat there and waited, hoping Cees didn't forget to make the call. She looked down at her watch and noticed that it was past the hour Cees said he would call, and Rita thought to herself that she must have missed her. That is, until the porch light came on. It took a few seconds, but Isis opened the door, stepping out onto the porch, anticipating Cees' car pulling up.

Rita went straight to work, and by the time Isis realized what was going on, it was too late. Rita let the Last Airbender go, sending a large number of bullets in Isis's direction, hitting everything on the porch except for Isis, who managed to take off into the house. Bullets chased her into the house, knocking holes in the living room walls the size of basketballs. The Sars 380 was bigger and louder than what Rita had expected. She had fired plenty of guns before, but this wasn't a gun that she could accurately manage due to the size of it.

Tossing the Last Airbender to the pavement, Rita grabbed the .40 cal from under her vest and ran into the house after her. She had to be cautious because she didn't know where Isis ran to or what kind of guns she had in the house, and at the same time, she had to be mindful of Shay being in the basement. The whole house got quiet, and Rita slow walked through the living room with her gun t-cupped in her hands. She took a mental note of her surroundings, first noticing the steps to the right that led upstairs. The lights in the kitchen were turned out, and Rita knew for sure Isis was going to pop up from out of the dark.

She was wrong. Isis had run upstairs when she first came into the house, making the choice to protect her daughter instead of using Shay as a hostage. It was her motherly instinct. Isis watched Rita from the top of the steps, but she couldn't get a good shot, because she could only see half of her body. She tried to creep down a couple steps with the Mossburg pump and get a good shot off, but the squeaky steps gave up her location to Rita, who spun around and started shooting up the stairs. She just missed Isis, who still got a shot off before retreating. The buckshot from the shot gun ripped a piece of the banister off the steps. Instead of retreating far, Isis ran back to the top of the steps and began firing the pump while at the same time walking down the steps, forcing Rita to take cover in the dining room.

Rita could hear Isis cocking the pump and the shell casings hitting the ground. The only thing that separated them was a thin wall Isis was waiting for Rita to come from behind.

"You don't gotta die like this, cousin," Isis yelled out from the steps, aiming the shotgun into the dark dining room.

"Bitch, I ain't got no rap. Come down off of those steps," Rita shot back, poppin' the clip out of her gun to check and see how many shots she had left, which was about seven or eight. Rita sat on the floor with her back against the wall, and she knew that she didn't have much time left before the police would be showing up. She had to make her move now, and she did. She reached around the wall and fired three quick shots in the direction of the steps.

It wasn't the bullets alone that made Isis run back up the steps. She could hear Briana calling for her, coming down the hallway. When Isis ran up the steps, Rita rolled over to her feet and shot up the steps behind her, letting off a shot and hitting Isis in the back of her leg.

She fell to the floor but kept the pump in her hand. Isis fired in the direction of the steps, seeing Rita's head peek over the top step. It missed Rita and hit the wall.

Briana stood next to Isis, crying at the top of her lungs, and it was at the point of trying to fire the pump again that she realized she was out of buck shots.

Now Rita's head peeked completely over the steps as she climbed them. Isis grabbed a hold of her daughter and tried to stop her from crying. Rita walked down the hallway with the .40 cal pointed right at Isis's face. She saw the little girl beside Isis, but it didn't slow Rita down one bit. She walked all the way up to Isis and pressed the gun up against her forehead, grabbing the little girl from out of her arms and putting her behind her, the whole while keeping eye contact with Isis.

"Please don't kill me in front of my daughter," Isis pleaded.

Rita didn't even pay that request any mind, squeezing the trigger and blowing Isis's brains all over the hallway wall. Her body fell to the floor, and Rita stood over her lifeless body and fired the remaining bullets into Isis's face until her gun goose-necked.

Briana was crying at the top of her lungs. She would be scarred for life with the vision of her mother being murdered so viciously in front of her. It would haunt her in her sleep. She would have visions of it at random times. It would affect every relationship she would try to have. She'd never be able to trust anyone. Her life's goal would be to get revenge for the murder of her mother.

Rita looked at Briana and left her there crying while she went downstairs to the basement.

Shay heard the door open, and she was still confused about what was going on upstairs. She thought that the kidnappers were trying to kill each other, or maybe even the police had found Isis, but when Rita came down the steps, she was overwhelmed with relief. Here she was, big sis, flying in to save the day.

"What? You look surprised to see me," Rita said, cutting the duct tape from around her feet.

Shay wanted to say something, but Rita was moving too fast, trying her best to get out of this house before the cops came, which she knew would be any second now. The only thing restraining Shay were the handcuffs. Rita didn't anticipate having to bring a key. It didn't matter anyway. Shay was up and running right behind Rita.

They got up the basement steps and headed for the front door, but when they ran past the steps, Shay noticed the little girl standing at the top of the stairs, staring right back at her with the saddest look on her face. Rita, who was already out the door, ran back in to see why Shay had stopped. She looked up the stairs to see the little girl putting her toy in her mouth. Shay looked at Rita.

Rita looked back at Shay, knowing what Shay was thinking. If Shay wasn't bound by handcuffs, she would have done it herself. Rita walked up the steps, and when she got right up on Briana, she stuck both of her arms out to pick her up. Briana was only two years old, but at that moment, she had to make the biggest decision of her life, and she did. She stuck her arms back out to Rita as though she wanted to go.

They all walked out of the house, fading off into the night, and it was in the nick of time, because the sound of police sirens was in the near distance. Home. That's where the girls were headed to.

Chapter 23

The lone gunman, who begged for his life, only received a bullet to the back of his head after Mozar and Seal bagged up everything in the safe. It had to be well over 100k in cash and about ten bricks of cocaine. They really didn't want to be sitting in a house with a dead body lying around, so the process of counting the money was going to have to wait. Rita really had come through on this deal, and everything looked like blue skies.

As Mozar and Seal were leaving the house, Mozar felt the hairs on the back of his neck stand up. He knew something was wrong off the break, and the first person he saw was a white man in a suit, pointing a gun at him from the bottom of the steps. He started to retreat back into the house, but the red beam sitting on his chest and the sound of the U.S. Marshal yelling at him from the adjacent porches had him thinking twice about moving at all. He was well aware of the consequences followed by any wrong movement, especially since he still had his gun in his hand.

"Drop the gun and get ya hands in the air," one of the U.S. Marshals yelled out, pointing an MP-5 directly at him.

Rita had set this whole thing up from the time Mozar robbed Shay and locked Dave up. She knew the type of cop he was and knew that his greed for money would be his demise. The day she met Mozar at the playground, Rita had stashed a tape recorder under the slide before he got there, so everything they talked about was recorded loud and clear. The anonymous call about where he could find Isis was just a decoy to keep him out of the way, so Rita would be able to do her thing.

The stash house she sent him to rob was a local drug dealer Rita use to beef wit' back in the day. She knew for sure that Mozar wasn't going to enter that house or exit it without getting into a shootout. Her hopes were for him to get killed during that shootout, but just in case he made it out of the house, she wanted to put him in another dilemma he was sure not to come out of.

The U.S. Marshal wasn't going to ask a second time for Mozar and Seal to drop their guns, and they both knew it. Seal had other things running through his mind. He surely wasn't trying to go down for the dead body in the house, and he definitely wasn't trying to go to prison for the rest of his life. Seal clutched his gun tighter, looking around to find who he was going to shoot first.

Mozar looked at him and could see suicide written all over his face. The two federal agents at the bottom of the steps could see Seal's hesitation as well.

"Don't do it. You don't have to go out like this," the agent yelled, tensing up with his gun pointed at Seal.

"Hold up, hold up. I'm dropping my gun," Mozar yelled out to the marshal, trying to take their attention off of Seal.

Seal didn't move. He just stood there with his gun still clutched in his hand. As bad as Mozar didn't want to go to prison himself, he wasn't ready to be gunned down like a wild animal. He was standing so close to Seal that every bullet that flew that way would have had to hit him before they hit Seal.

"Nooo, Nooo," Mozar yelled out, pointing at certain marshals that looked like they were ready to start firing. "He's not going to do anything," he screamed, trying to lower the tension in the air. "We can't go out like this," he told Seal, looking at him with sincerity in his eyes.

Silence took over, and for a moment, the marshals knew that they were going to have to put Seal down. Seal's eyes filled up with tears at the thought of going to jail and leaving behind his family. He really wanted to die, but he didn't want to force the marshals to have to kill his partner in the process.

Seal dropped the gun on the ground and put his hands in the air slowly. Mozar sighed in relief, putting his hands in the air, somewhat relieved that it was over. As the marshals started to close in, Mozar was the first to get down on the ground and lay flat on his stomach. He was waiting to see Seal follow him to the ground, but when he didn't, Mozar just closed his eyes and braced himself for the worst.

Seal waited until the marshals got a little bit closer before he quickly reached into his back pocket and pulled out a .38. The marshals reached swiftly, but not swiftly enough.

"Gun, gun!" one of the marshals yelled out.

It was too late. Seal got a shot off, striking the Marshal who yelled in the neck. The return fire was catastrophic. Every officer out there fired upon Seal, hitting him in every part of his body that was visible. It took a split second, and by the time Mozar got a chance to look up after all the shooting had subsided, he was looking right into the bloody, half shredded face of his partner. Now, Mozar knew exactly what it felt like to be amongst the wolves. One up for the street, and game over for the police.

Final Chapter

Rita sat in the hospital room, reading an urban novel called *Drake* out loud so that David might be able to hear her voice and hopefully wake up. Shay and Briana were there as well, keeping Rita company most of the time. Dave had been in a coma ever since the shooting, and every day since, Rita had been right next to his side. The doctors were optimistic about Dave waking up in the near future, and the first person she wanted him to see was her. No drug selling, no partying, no nothing. Everything was on hold, and the streets of West Philly were feeling the effects of it.

Rita couldn't get it out of her mind about what happened that night and the reasons why it happened, and nobody, not even Shay, could understand how she felt. She looked up at the monitor as it continued to beep, checking Dave's vital signs every so often. All she could think about was Dave's description of what the word "love" meant to him, and how his description coincided with his actions. He put his life on the line for her, and for that, she felt forever indebted to him.

"You know how much loyalty means to me and how I live by it," Rita began. "But, Shay, I'ma teach you something that was taught to me by a very smart man. Sometimes in life, when you love someone and that love is real, you have to no longer live for yourself. You sacrifice everything in order to share that everything with the person you love. Mc, I'm sacrificing right now, and until the day the man that I'm in love with so much wakes up out of his coma, I'ma be sitting right here, waiting."

Out of nowhere, Cees walked into the room with his baby son in his arms. He looked a lot different from the condition Rita and Shay had met him. He had a look of humbleness on his face, and when he spoke, it sounded submissive. All kinds of thoughts ran through Rita's head, but not the kind she expected. She thought that she would want to kill Cees after all that she and Shay had been through. She never thought that she would be able to sit in the same room as him, but the truth of the matter was Cees was only doing what was in his nature, and at the end of the day, his heart changed, just like Dave's did. What happened was part of the game when you're in it, and it's only but so long one can play the game until he figures out that games are for children.

What further caught Rita's immediate attention was how Shay didn't show any signs of anger or aggression toward Cees. After all that she'd been through, if anybody would have any animosity in their hearts, it would be Shay. But she didn't show one sign of it. Rita even managed to see Shay smile, something that definitely wasn't expected, when Cees asked her how she was doing. She didn't know that Shay and Cees actually built somewhat of a friendship during the time she was held captive, and Shay had vowed to stand by more than her word that she wasn't going to kill Cees if she saw him in the streets.

Cees took a seat in the corner. His baby on his lap, he looked out the window at the city. Shay came over and pulled a chair up next to him. She sat with Briana in her lap. She looked out the window with Cees. Cees looked over at Shay, and Shay looked at Cees. She reached out and took Cees' hand in hers. They smiled at each other, then both looked out the window again, smiling. Briana snuggled into Shay.

Rita was right next to Dave, holding his hand and praying. She prayed to God that if Dave woke up, she'd be done with the streets. She'd devote her life to making things right and taking care of Dave, whatever that would be. Just as she finished her prayer, she thought she saw a flutter in Dave's eye. She thought it might just be the tears in her eyes playing tricks. She wiped her eyes to make sure. She saw the flutter again. Then, with no warning, Dave opened his eyes.

Tears silently fell from Rita's eyes. She had never smiled so big in her entire life. When Dave's eyes finally adjusted, he saw Rita.

Rita could see Dave's smile behind his breathing tube. "You're awake," she said through happy tears.

Cees and Shay turned around instantly. Seeing Dave's eyes open, they rushed to the side of his bed.

Dave looked over at Cees holding his godson and Shay holding a little girl, and at that point, he knew that he was in store for a good story.

"Hey, mister," Rita said with the biggest smile on her face she could have. "I missed you."

Dave looked around the room, satisfied with what he was seeing. He tried to talk and realized he had a breathing tube. If he could, he would have said how happy he was to see all of his favorite people together. He was for sure happy. Happy that he was surrounded by his new family, a family that was built on trust, and a family that was based on loyalty.

Also by Marcus Weber

Carl Weber's Kingpins:

The Bronx

Prologue

"Are you ready?"

Paige looked up, startled. She blinked a few times and looked to her right and smiled. "I guess so," she replied, jamming her right fist into her hip, with her arm bent at the elbow to make an opening for her brother to slide his arm through.

"You look amazing, sis."

Paige's stomach clenched. Her father had said almost those exact words the first time she'd gotten married. *You look amazing, baby girl.*

A small explosion of heat lit in Paige's chest—one part anger, one part sadness—as she thought about her father's nerve when he refused to give her away a second time. She closed her eyes and exhaled. She shook her head, wishing away her worries. She couldn't focus on the past right now. If she did, she might not make it down the aisle this time. And this time, the marriage was a necessity, not just a want.

"You clean up nicely yourself." Paige looked up at her brother, her fake smile perfected now.

It was true. Gladstone Tillary, Jr., had come a long way since his latest stint in rehab. Even with his neck tattoos peeking from his shirt collar, he presented well—classy and sharp. Paige was sorry she'd ever gotten him involved in everything that had happened. Her heart broke every time she thought about how she had turned her back on him in his darkest hour, yet he had stood by her in hers.

"I really appreciate you getting rid of those awful dreadlocks, too," she said, her tone playful.

"Well, they're gone but not forgotten," her brother joked, running his hand over his neatly trimmed hair.

They laughed.

Paige needed the laugh. She'd take anything to ease some of the muscle-twisting tension that had her entire body in knots.

Finally, the low hum of her wedding song, *You* by Kenny Latimore, filtered through the outdoor speakers.

"That's our cue."

Her brother squared his shoulders and tightened his lock on Paige's arm, forcing her closer to him.

"Thank you for being here, Junior," Paige whispered. She meant it. She knew he'd probably endured a harsh berating from their parents for agreeing to give her away. That was the one quality she had always admired most about her baby brother since they were kids. He never cared what her parents said or thought, unlike Paige, who had spent her entire life walking the fine line of being an individual and making her parents happy. She always wanted to be the "good one," as her mother called her.

"C'mon. You know I wouldn't miss the free food and wine," her brother joked.

Paige giggled. Then she got serious. "No wine for you," she chastised in a playfully gruff voice.

"All right. Here we go."

Paige looked down and smoothed her left hand over the fine, hand-sewn iridescent beads on the front of her haute couture gown. She found a lone bead to pick at with the hopes it would help calm her nerves.

"Loosen up. You're a pro at this, right? Sec‹
the charm?"

Paige parted a quivery-lipped smile. "The
shaking you'd think this was my first time."

She sucked in her breath as she finally stoo‹
end of the beautifully decorated aisle in the p‹
Breaux Vineyard. One-hundred-year-old weepi›
lows swayed in the wake of the breeze with their
white bud covered tendrils calling her forward. Pink
petals dotted the path in the center aisle, and tall s
stanchions holding white and lilac hydrangea glo
flanked every other row of white Chiavari chairs. Drea
romantic, and heavenly were all words that came to mir.

With her arm hooked through her brother's, Paig
plastered on her famous, toothy smile and carefull‹
navigated the vineyard's emerald green lawn in her heels
Collective awestruck gasps rose and fell amongst the
guests seated on either side of the decorated bridal path.
The absence of her parents and her best friend, Michaela,
didn't go unnoticed. But, it was the Cartwrights—Emil,
Hayden, and Jackson—who caused Paige to stumble a bit.

Focus, Paige. Focus. She knew they were there to
make sure she went through with it, their presence like a
threat whispered in her ear. *It'll all be over soon,* she told
herself.

Antonio stepped into the aisle to meet her. He wore a
smile that said, "I'm trying to make this seem real too."
Unlike Paige's penchant for the grandiose, Antonio was
simple. He wore a plain black suit, forgoing the obliga-
tory tuxedo, white cummerbund, and shiny shoes.

Paige felt something flutter inside her like a million
butterflies trapped in a jar. With everything they'd been
through, Paige had lost sight of how handsome Antonio
was. He looked more gorgeous now than he had years ago

eral huddles of them. One cluster almost the exact clone of the next. They all wore the biggest earrings dangling from their ears and the shortest, tightest skirts Paige had ever seen on young girls. And, she'd never, ever, seen fishnet stockings, except on women on television in those 80s movies she and Michaela liked to watch and laugh at. The girls were loud, and their body language was flirtatious. If it weren't for their baby faces, Paige would have pegged them for prostitutes like the ones she had seen in those movies.

Paige looked over at Michaela. "Obviously we are not dressed for this. Do you see that girl's nails? They look like neon green claws, while we're wearing boring French manicures. Way off, Michaela."

"I know, which means we will stand out. Don't you know anything? Look at them," Michaela said and jerked her chin at the girls. "The boys are used to them. Just look how they're trying to get attention, and the boys are all ignoring them. They won't be used to us, which means they'll be all over us. Now come on and stop being scared."

As soon as Paige and Michaela walked into the packed party, Paige started coughing. The thick, gray haze of smoke mixed with cheap colognes and drugstore perfumes was enough to require a gas mask. It didn't faze Michaela.

"Look, but don't be obvious. Ahead . . . 2 o'clock," Michaela yelled in Paige's ear over the booming music.

"What? Another bunch of boys?" Paige asked.

"No, silly! *These* boys are from Wings Academy, the number-one-ranked high school basketball team in the nation," Michaela corrected. "They are future stars!"

Paige shrugged. Neither she nor Michaela needed to be worried about snagging a basketball star. Both of them came from wealthy families. There would be several fifteen-hundred-dollar-per-plate social events their parents would drag them to where they'd be expected to find their future husbands, and they would definitely not be high school basketball players with dreams of being rich. They'd already be rich, from birth.

"Are you crazy, Paige? I hear basketball star dick is the best," Michaela said, pumping her pelvis in and out so Paige would understand.

"Ew. Stop. Just stop." Paige shook her head.

"Virgin," Michaela teased, waving at her.

They laughed.

"No, but seriously, Paige, one of them is looking over here," Michaela had pointed out. "He seems like the star. Look at the girls over there pointing at him. Maybe he wants me."

Paige had already spotted him. Michaela was wrong. For once, a boy was staring at Paige and not Michaela. Paige had felt his eyes on her as soon as she'd waved her vision clear of the thick smoke fog. He was so tall it was hard not to notice him. Even in the dark room, Paige had also noticed that he was teenage-movie-star handsome.

"He's coming this way!" Michaela shouted and bounced like she was about to see her favorite celebrity heartthrob. "Is my hair okay?"

Paige blinked a few times, trying to get her eyes to focus, but within seconds the handsome stranger was standing in front of her. No time to primp or even make sure her hair was okay.

"You want to dance?" he asked, his voice deep with unexpected bass.

Paige's heart throttled upward until she felt like it was caught in her throat. She opened her mouth, but no sound would come out.

Michaela pushed Paige forward before she could answer. "Yes, she does."

"I'm Antonio," he said, holding out his hand.

228 Marcus Weber

"Pa . . . Paige," she replied, putting her hand into his.

If Antonio remembered the day that he and Michaela met, he would have to think about how he ended up at that party in the first place. Growing up in the Patterson Houses meant that Antonio actively tried to stay away from functions big enough to cause problems, but his boy, Rich, had insisted.

"Deadass, G, there's going to be so many fine bitches," Rich had said as Antonio laid on his couch earlier that night. He had just finished practice and was more concerned with making sure he got up early enough to hit the gym again in the morning.

"Man, chill, no one cares about that. You not fucking anyway," Antonio said, grabbing the remote off the couch and turning on the T.V.

Rich moved to the set and turned it off. They had been friends for so long, he had spent so much time in Antonio's living room that he didn't even have to look to do it. While Rich didn't grow up in the same projects that Antonio did, he always found his way around and kept Antonio from getting his ass beat every time he curved the gang members who tried to recruit him.

"Well we sure as hell not fucking here, either," Rich said. "May as well up our chances." He smiled in the mischievous way that Antonio recognized meant that he was about to make a dumbass decision, and he was going to take him down with him. Antonio sighed.

"Fuck it, let's go."

Rich and Antonio got to the party twenty minutes before Michaela and Paige did. Like most parties that Rich peer-pressured his friend into going to, the function on Fordham Road was the usual cross between teenage gang bangers trying to sell to the kids from the high schools in the area and the kids from out in Riverdale who thought it would be cute to slum it for a minute. When Rich first saw Michaela and Paige, he knew what category they belonged to, and as he saw his friend's eyes land on Paige and stay there, he snapped his fingers in front of his eyes.

"Yo, nah, don't do that," said Rich. "Ain't nothing over there that you want." He grabbed Antonio's chin and tried to tear his gaze away from what he knew were just two bougie bitches trying to spice up their typical Friday night scene. Antonio clicked his tongue and hit his hand away.

"Boy, don't touch me," Antonio said and turned his eyes back onto the pretty girl who looked like she was trying to go to a business meeting. Rich rolled his eyes. He knew Antonio's type.

"Just because you like to pretend you're not from here doesn't mean they will," he said under his breath, and Antonio, who had actually heard him, ignored it. But that's when Frank, one of those dudes who had dropped out of school at fourteen and looked the part, came to stand in between Antonio and his target for the night.

"What's good?" Frank said to Antonio and Rich, which was bold considering everyone in the neighborhood knew that Antonio didn't entertain delinquency. No one seemed to understand why it was that Antonio was so actively trying to avoid being caught up. It wasn't like it was uncommon for people to sell or to smoke or to do any number of illicit activities. To everyone else, it looked like Antonio just thought he was better than them, that just because he could hoop meant he was something special. But to Antonio, it was more than that.

Even though he didn't know a lot about his father, Antonio knew that he must have been a stand-up dude the way his mother talked about him, the way she kept his name out of her mouth unlike the other single mothers on their block. And because of this, he decided he would keep his head up and out of the streets, no matter how bad things got, or how much money he and his mom went without. He knew in his heart one day his skills with the ball would pay off.

"Get the fuck on, Frank," said Rich. He knew about Antonio's deep disregard for gang life, and even though he found Antonio's fronting annoying sometimes, he supported his friend first. Frank laughed, having expected that reaction, and walked away, bringing Paige back into Antonio's eye line.

"She's breathtaking," Antonio told Rich quietly, not even noticing that her friend was whispering in her ear while staring in their direction.

"You're mad corny. Just go talk to her. You look creepy staring at her like that," said Rich.

Antonio shook his shoulders out and smoothed his eyebrows, and then he crossed the room toward what he now realized were two girls and not one. He could handle women the way he handled a basketball: with delicate finesse before making his shot. As he stood in front of her and looked down, he noticed how pretty her eyes were.

"You want to dance?"

Without realizing it, Antonio said the words from his memory out loud, and Paige blinked a few times, remembering where she was. The wedding ceremony was a blur. It was not until cheers erupted from the small crowd of sixty guests that Paige realized it was done. She'd married Antonio for the second time. To hell with the reasons they had divorced in the first place. The reasons . . . Thinking about the reasons made Paige think of Michaela, whose absence at the wedding was as noticeable as a huge sinkhole in the middle of the widely traveled road.

Paige felt sick, but still, she flashed a smile.

"And now I can kiss my bride," Antonio beamed, playing his role. Paige welcomed his tongue into her mouth for a long, passionate seal of their vows. It didn't matter what she felt. She knew it would make for better headlines in the media. Better ratings, too. It would also set her in-laws at ease. Remarrying Antonio needed to solve their problems. It needed to save their lives. It needed to right all of the wrongs. It needed to keep her from having to testify against him . . . them.

Antonio and Paige pulled apart and turned toward their spectators. Cheers arose. Paige's cheeks flushed, and the bones in her face ached from grinning. She deserved an Academy Award.

Antonio wore a cool grin as they slowly made their way down the aisle. He squeezed Paige's hand as if to say, "at least this part is over."

"Wait right there . . . hold that pose!" the photographer called out. "Kiss her," he instructed, hoisting his camera to eye level to ensure he captured the exact moment their lips met. The flash exploded around them. Cameras rolled. Money shot after money shot was captured. This was great.

Paige and Antonio turned to each other on cue, their tongues engaged in another scandalously intimate dance. The photographer's flash lit up in front of them like heavenly beams of light, and the crowd erupted in another round of cheers. Perfection.

The sun basked the couple in abundant light and warmth. It was truly the perfect May afternoon for an outdoor wedding. If only everything else in their lives were this perfect.

"Walk slowly forward now," the photographer instructed, the camera crew backing up for the wide angled shots.

When Paige and Antonio finally made it to the end of the aisle, they were bombarded by guests eager to snap photos with cell phones and personal cameras. Noticing the paparazzi disguised as regular guests, Antonio waved like a politician and Paige flashed her debutante smile. Everyone wanted to get the story first.

"Antonio." Jackson Cartwright stepped into their path, clapping his hand on Antonio's shoulder.

Paige's smile faded, and she bit down into her jaw.

"I didn't think you'd go through with it. I'm proud of you. Maybe you're braver than I thought," Jackson said, smiling. He turned his attention to Paige. "Congratulations."

Paige shivered.

"One more!" the photographer shouted, jutting his camera forward for a close-up.

Paige twisted away, happy for the distraction. Antonio and Paige faced each other, their fake happiness hanging over them like a freshly blown bubble. He kissed her chastely on the nose. She giggled at his playfulness. What a performance! Paige pictured them standing hand-in-hand on a stage, accepting a Tony Award for best actor and actress.

"Antonio!" a voice boomed.

Paige's head whipped left, then right. It was hard to determine what direction the voice had come from until it sounded again. This time, louder. More sinister.

Antonio's head jerked to the left. Paige craned her neck, but there were so many people in front of them.

"Antonio!" the voice boomed again. "You should've played by the rules!" Screams erupted as the wedding goers saw the source of the voice first.

"Oh my God! Gun! He's got a gun!" a guest screamed.

Antonio's eyes widened. Frantically, he unhooked his arm from Paige's and stepped in front of her. Before he could make another move, the sound of rapid-fire explosions cut through the air.

Chapter 1

Fool's Gold

One year earlier

Paige nodded at the hostess and attempted a smile. "Broadwell party," she huffed. She exhaled and tucked her hair behind her left ear. She could feel the perspiration tickling her top lip, but wiping it would smear her freshly beat face. There was no meeting the ladies without a flawless face of makeup.

Paige shifted her weight on her heels as the hostess scanned her list.

"It should be under Michaela Broadwell. I'm kind of late." Paige craned her neck to see if she spotted Michaela in the restaurant, so she could save the hostess some time and point Michaela out.

"Ah, yes. Broadwell. Party of four," the hostess sang like she'd just discovered something great. "Right this way."

Paige followed, rehearsing believable excuses in her head.

Sorry girl, but just as I was walking out, Christian got sick.

Girl, blame my mother. She called with her usual melodrama, and I lost track of time listening to her complain.

Sorry to have you waiting. The nanny called out, and I had to get a sitting service last minute.

Paige could live with picking one of those excuses—anything other than the real reason she was late. She could imagine the slight hint of satisfaction masked as concern that would crop up on Michaela's face if she knew what really happened. Paige envisioned Michaela sucking in her breath and her cat-green eyes going round. "Oh, Paige. I'm so sorry this is happening to you," Michaela would say sympathetically, as if Paige had just told her she had cancer. Paige swallowed hard. That would make her sick. She hated people to pity her.

Paige loved Michaela, but they'd always had a mildly competitive relationship. As kids, if Paige got a new bike, Michaela would beg her parents for a bigger, prettier, fancier bike. As teens, if Paige got a new piece of jewelry from her father, like the diamond tennis bracelet she got at her sweet sixteen, Michaela would be sure to get the bracelet, earrings, and necklace. Even as adults, when Paige's relationship with Antonio got serious, Michaela killed herself to find an athlete who could measure up, though Michaela's mother had wanted her to marry Barry Richardson, a future lawyer whose parents were wealthy.

All of that aside, Paige loved Michaela. Paige couldn't imagine her life without Michaela. Without her, who would she tell her deepest secrets? Who would give her advice? Who would be her voice when she lost hers, which was often? Michaela always had Paige's back, and even when social anxiety kept Paige from speaking up for herself in certain situations, Michaela would step in and be her mouthpiece.

"Here we are," the hostess said, extending her hand toward the seat like a church usher. "I'll leave the menu here for you. Enjoy ladies."

"Thank you," Paige huffed, plunking her bag down in the empty chair next to hers.

Before she could sit down, Michaela was on her. "Thank you for gracing me with your presence, Mrs. Roberts," Michaela sniped, tapping the top of her sparkly, diamond-encrusted Rolex, another "out-do Paige" item.

"I know. I know."

"You know, alright. You know I do not like looking like a chick on a blind date that got stood up," Michaela complained with the strained chuckle that meant she was annoyed but trying. She stood up, and they exchanged a perfunctory hug and cheek-to-cheek air kiss.

Michaela looked beautiful as usual. Paige admired how Michaela kept her skin glowing all year around like she was fresh off of a Caribbean beach vacation every day.

"Just been a crazy day," Paige said, her voice clipped. She didn't bother to offer one of her practiced excuses. Michaela knew her too well.

"You know I wanted to have some time alone with you before the other girls got here." Michaela looked at her watch again. "Shit, now we only have about twenty minutes to chat before the gossip hound and the preacher's wife arrive."

"I'm sorry," Paige said, leaving it at that. She picked up a glass of water with already melted ice and sipped, hoping it would settle her stomach.

"So, what's up, girl?" Paige let Michaela start talking about what was going on with her. That always did the trick when Paige wanted to forget her own problems. Michaela loved to have the spotlight, and Paige loved to give it to her.

"There's so much happening," Michaela lowered her voice and leaned in closer to the table, her green eyes wide like what she had to say was top secret.

Paige uncurled her toes and let her shoulders drop. For the first time in hours, she relaxed. There was always so much happening with Michaela. She would forever be one of those spoiled rich girls who believed every small thing was a huge deal. Michaela could make a garden snake into a boa constrictor, or a campfire into a raging inferno. But, the one thing Paige had always admired about her best friend was her fearlessness. Michaela was fearless in a way that would make her jump in the face of a six-foot-tall hulk of a man in a road rage incident and punch him in the face without blinking an eye.

"So, hurry up and fill me in," Paige urged. Anything to keep Michaela from asking her about what was going on in her life.

"Well, Rod is retiring. But, you already know that. So, I'm in the process of planning the party. I think it'll be good for him. A change. A break from his . . . you know . . . grief."

Paige nodded. She wanted to ask so badly if Michaela really thought right now was a good time in Rod's life for a party. His brother had just been murdered and dragged through the mud as a drug-dealing gangbanger in the media. But the excitement in Michaela's voice made Paige stay silent.

"Oh my God, that party planner—Minted Events—has the best ideas. Shayna, the owner, flew in all the way from Houston just to show me samples of what she has. Now, that's customer service. And, I'm scouring all of the top designers for my dress. It has to be two seasons ahead, or else it simply won't work," Michaela prattled.

Paige nodded and sipped her water. Just envisioning any over-the-top event Michaela would throw made Paige feel like sinking into the floor. She thought she could put her worries aside for this lunch with the ladies, but she hadn't considered that their usual pretentious banter would send her mind racing, worrying. Would she even be able to afford a designer dress for Michaela's husband's retirement party? Who would be there? Would there be a red carpet? Paparazzi? Would everyone know what happened by then?

"I have to find him a suit, because you know Rod. He'll show up in a hoodie and sweats if I don't reel him in. After all these years with this beauty as a wife, he is still like the beast—"

"Antonio got let go from another team." Paige didn't know why, but the words just bubbled out of her. Her stomach contracted. Saying the words gave Paige the kind of relief you felt after vomiting. She gulped her water this time, wishing it were a stiff drink. And she didn't even drink.

Michaela's eyebrows shot up into arches, and she flattened her right hand over her heart. "Oh, Paige. I'm so sorry."

Paige had almost had her words down perfectly.

"He says we'll be okay. They bought out the contract, and he's going to invest the money," Paige said, trying to convince herself, more than Michaela, that her lifestyle would stay the same and that she wouldn't be explaining things to her parents . . . again.

"You don't have to give up your house, do you?" Michaela gasped like she was asking if Paige had to have both of her lungs removed. "And what about Christian . . . will he have to change schools? What about your parents? What will they say? Will you ask them for help? Will you get a job?" Michaela shot questions at her, rapid fire.

Paige blanched. She had already asked herself all of those questions when Antonio came home, half drunk, and woke her with the news. Paige had sat up in the bed, her black velvet sleep mask pulled up on her forehead, and sleep clouding her brain. She listened to Antonio rant about how it had happened this time.

"They were all standing around in Dan's office, all smug and shit," Antonio had griped, sitting at her side, hunched over with his elbows on his knees and his fists clenched.

"Of course Dan hid behind his fancy, big-dog desk like a coward. Couldn't even hold eye contact with me. They acted like I needed a handout or some shit. I played my ass off for that team. Everybody knows I got at least three more good years on the court."

Paige swung her legs over the side of the bed and got closer to him. She'd contemplated hugging him, but didn't.

"Can you believe Dan spoke to me like I was one of those kids who'd tried out for the team but didn't make it? 'Tony, you've been a pleasure to work with. All of us . . . the entire organization has nothing but respect and admiration for you. We think you're a great guy and personally, I think you're one of the best guards I know. But we have to move in a different direction. These young players are a new breed, stronger, faster, and we have to be able to compete,'" Antonio repeated general manager Dan Sidelman's words almost verbatim. When he was done, Antonio moved his tongue over his bottom lip, like uttering the words had left behind a painful, oozing blister.

Paige lowered her eyes to her trembling hands. She wanted to be supportive. For goodness sake, she could see the disappointment hiding behind Antonio's anger. She had also sensed that it was different from the look she had seen Antonio wear every time he'd been traded or let go before. Paige knew it was the end of Antonio's basketball career. She had felt a prickling sense of horror like some dreadful poverty monster would jump out of her closet and snatch her up.

"What will we do?" she'd asked, her fear making her unable to bring herself to hug him or offer any comfort.

Antonio had blown out a windstorm of breath, braced himself, and stood up from the bed. "I'll work it out," he said, rubbing his chin like he always did when he was thinking. "Things aren't going to just fall apart overnight. I'll invest everything I have left and make it grow. I know plenty of people that can help me make money."

Paige had taken in a deep, shaky breath. She hadn't wanted to press. She wasn't the nagging type, but she shuddered at the thought of going through another tough financial time waiting for a team to pick Antonio up. Just thinking about going through that again made the hairs on her neck stand up. Thinking of all of the pretending she would have to do in front of her friends and family was what twisted her insides into knots the most. And her son—he deserved to live like she had as a child.

Paige had looked around her expansive bedroom and wondered how they were going to maintain their lifestyle this time. Would it be an unauthorized loan from her brother's trust fund, again? Would she go behind Antonio's back and ask her mother again? Would she pawn off a few handbags, jewelry? Or would she leave this time?

"That's what you said before, and we almost lost everything," Paige blurted out. She'd wanted to be supportive. She really did. She felt a pang of guilt for saying it, but she didn't take it back. This time, she couldn't back her words.

Antonio tipped his head back and stared at the ceiling with a clenched jaw. "Don't worry, Paige. I won't let you be embarrassed because you can't spend ten thousand dollars on a bag or take a European vacation for two-fucking-weeks. God forbid. I'd rather kill myself first," he shot back.

"Don't take your frustrations out on me, Antonio. This impacts me too. We have a child in private school. Music lessons. Tennis lessons. Rowing. We have this house. And, what about all of the cars? What will people think if we have to downgrade our lifestyle?"

Antonio chortled a deep, guttural sound full of contradiction to the scowl on his face. "Wow. Really, Paige? That's what you're going with?" Antonio said and shook his head in disgust. "Everything you just mentioned was material shit. Every. Single. Thing." He slapped the balled fingers on his right hand into the palm of his left as he said the last three words. "Do you even realize the shit that runs your life? You have no other purpose, do you? Impressing the world—that's it, huh? Like mother, like daughter? Living for what others think of you? No real identity?"

Paige had sprung to her feet, his words a gut-punch. She'd folded her arms across her chest to stave off the ache she felt in her belly.

"What else is there to think about in a time like this? Obviously, all of these years, my purpose has been to make sure you don't fuck up our lives, Antonio. I've stuck by you through things that most women would've bailed out on a long time ago. Remember that. That's love. You never wanted me to work. You never want me to go to my parents for anything. You always want to pretend you've got it. I'm not going to pretend with you this time," Paige had said in her chilliest voice. The gloves had certainly come off. She regretted the words as soon as she'd said them, but it had been too late. She hated being like that with him. And, she knew how sensitive Antonio was about living up to her parent's standards.

"Right, I know. I pretend." Antonio threw his hands up. "Yes, that's it. I pretend that you spend thousands of dollars a month with no regard for where it came from or is coming from. I pretend that your parents are always secretly judging me because no matter how good you live, no matter how much I give you, I will always be that poor kid from the projects that just happened to make it out of the hood . . . never good enough for the senator's daughter, no matter what. I also pretend I don't know you regret losing your trust fund because you fell in love with me. And, most-of-fucking-all, Paige, I pretend that you would've married me even if I wasn't on my way to the League!" Antonio had exploded.

"Stop it! I didn't mean it like that," Paige yelled as tears danced down her flushed cheeks. How had she meant it?

"Look," Antonio had exhaled, softening.

She knew that he hated to see her cry. He hated to disappoint her. He'd said that probably one thousand times during their marriage.

"I said I would work it out, and I will."

"Hey, ladies!" the shrill southern drawl broke up Paige's thoughts and ended Michaela's barrage of what-will-you-do questions.

Michaela's face, which had just a second ago been dragged down with pity for Paige, was suddenly jovial. "Koi! It's so good to see you!"

Paige shifted in her seat at how easy it was for Michaela to change moods. Paige imagined that this talent of Michaela's must've been a gift and a curse.

"Paigey," Koi sang, pushing on Paige's shoulder.

Paige wanted to vomit, but she plastered on a fake smile, pushed away from the table, and stood up.

Let the pretending begin.

"Wait, have you lost weight? Girl, you are so beautiful. The lighting in this place is doing it for those gray eyes," Koi gushed in her annoying sing-songy-Paula-Deen voice. She tapped cheeks with Paige. A real Southern belle.

"I know I say this every time, but you two, with that ashy blond hair, that buttery skin that you both seem to be able to keep so radiant all year 'round, and those colored eyes . . . green and gray is it . . . always make me think of twins . . . sisters, at least," Koi gushed. "Yes, twins. There has to be some family connection. It's just too strange."

Is she going to say that every time she sees us? Paige wondered, annoyed.

People always asked Paige and Michaela if they were sisters, and when they'd say no, they'd ask, "Cousins, at least?"

Paige guessed it was because ignorant people thought it so rare that two black girls, friends no less, could have fair skin, dusty blond hair, and colored eyes.

Paige and Michaela had also discussed Koi's obsession with their looks. Paige opined that Koi was uncomfortable with her own coffee-bean complexion, which she noticeably tried to lighten with the wrong, way-too-light shade of foundation. There was nothing about Koi that Paige really thought was endearing, but she put up with her for the sake of Michaela and to say she had friends. It was just what socialites did—maintain fake friendships, meet and eat, and spend money on things that boosted their reputations.

Every time they met up, Paige thought, *Who named their child Koi?* Wasn't that the name of those hideous orange, red, and silver fish that swam around in the neat little decorative ponds of rich people who thought they brought them good feng shui?

Koi was married to Damien Armstrong, former criminal-turned-pastor of Full of Life Ministries, a megachurch in Westchester. Koi was far from what Paige would've considered first lady-like. Growing up, Paige watched the first lady of her family's church sit quietly in the front pew wearing an angelic smile, dressed in almost floor-length paisley dresses with lace-trimmed collars that covered her collarbone, and she spoke in mousy, hushed murmurs while church members always seemed to be fussing over her. The total opposite of Koi, who never left home in anything other than the brightest, tightest, above-the-knee dresses with so much cleavage-spillage she could probably double as a circus sideshow—the megachurch first lady who could balance a Bible on her breasts. Koi spoke loudly as if she was always on a stage commanding an audience's attention. She lived for attention. And, did first ladies wear so much weave and outlandish clown-like makeup? Today's choice was a purple, glittery eyeshadow and shiny fuchsia lipstick.

At that moment, Paige was a bit annoyed by Koi's presence. She was just another person to make Paige feel like her life was in shambles.

"You know, in all of my years in New York, I've never come to this place. Heard about it, never got around to it. Damien is so busy all the time. With his flock of believers growing each week, date nights have become few and far between," Koi said as she looked around in wide-eyed amazement.

Paige smirked. "I'm surprised. You're so . . . you know . . . worldly, and this place has been around forever."

La Grenouille was a well-known celebrity haunt in Manhattan that Michaela always felt was worth making appearances at, so they visited often. Paige loved the rustic, yet modern ambiance. The wooden walls, the traditional furniture that still looked new, the bouquets of fresh flowers, and classic light fixtures gave the inside of the restaurant a suave, chic feel.

"I love it here. Caught quite a few juicy news tidbits in this place," Casey announced, approaching from the side like she'd been part of the conversation all along.

Paige, Michaela, and Koi all seemed to look up at the same time with simultaneous raised-brow, mouth-agape surprise.

"Hey girls," Casey sang. "How did y'all know exactly where to sit? This is my favorite table. This is the perfect spot. Front and center. I can enjoy and still see if any celebrities bounce in on the creep. You all know I love a good, juicy story."

"It's so rude to sneak up on people," Michaela grumbled at Casey without bothering to stand up. Koi gave Casey a weak air kiss and a flat, "Hey, girl." Paige stood and gave Casey a tight hug.

Michaela sighed heavily and picked up her menu. Paige shot her a stern look. She was starting to believe that Michaela was jealous of her friendship with Casey.

"We haven't ordered anything while we waited for you. I'm starving, so can you sit down," Michaela griped with a passive aggressive smile.

"I sure can," Casey replied, overly cheery. She pulled out the chair next to Paige.

Michaela exhaled loudly.

Casey's arrival made Paige feel better. Someone normal, finally. Casey didn't have it as good financially as they all did, but she had become a good source of information since she was one of the most popular gossip bloggers on the web, and Paige thought she was more genuine than most of the women in the social elite of the New York City scene. There was something pure about Casey that Paige couldn't quite place, but it was endearing just the same. Paige didn't know if it was Casey's deep cheek dimples, which made her look like an innocent-faced baby cherub, or if it was that Casey didn't care to pretend like they all did. Casey was full figured and was never one to eat bird food or pretend she was trying to lose weight.

Casey also wasn't as materialistic and showy as the rest of them. Casey proudly rocked her Michael Kors bags, when the others wouldn't be caught dead with Michael Kors anything. Paige admired that a man didn't define Casey. Casey made her own money from her celebrity gossip blog and the burgeoning online boutique for big girls that she owned. She lived by her own rules and was always proud to say that she was single and ready to mingle—a luxury Paige had never been afforded, since she'd given herself solely to Antonio since high school.

Michaela and Paige had had a few spats over Paige's friendship with Casey. Paige had put Michaela in her place once. "I don't know what you have against this girl. Just because you don't know what it is like to be new to any situation, no friends, no support, doesn't mean everyone is like you. Give her a chance. She's smart and independent. We could learn a thing or two from her," Paige had chided.

"So, what's good on the menu?" Koi asked as she scanned her leather-bound menu like it was hard to read.

"I like everything. You can't go wrong in classy restaurants," Michaela replied without looking up from her menu.

"Good evening, ladies," a tall, slender, handsome young waiter approached. "I'm Anwar, and I'll be serving you this evening."

"Mmm. An-war." Koi licked her lips and sized him up. "I can appreciate a young prince named after an African leader," Koi said, pushing up her already bulging cleavage.

Paige wanted to throw her water on Koi to cool her down. Again, more un-first-lady-like behavior.

"I'll start with a Cosmo," Michaela ordered first.

"Hennessy sidecar for me," Koi went next.

A first lady drinking Hennessy?

"For me . . . something light and fruity. I don't drink," Paige said.

"My usual, Anwar," Casey chimed in, winking at the waiter.

Michaela sucked her teeth, and Koi grunted. Paige lowered her head and smiled.

By the time the food came, all of the ladies had loosened up. Even Paige had forgotten her fight with Antonio for the time being. In some strange way, the chatter, the ebb and flow of stomach-hurting laughter, and even the masked bitchiness and blatant competitiveness that hovered over the table, brought Paige some comfort. She'd looked around at every single one of her friends and thought, at that moment, she was like fool's gold, all shiny and believable on the surface, when deep down she felt fake and worthless.

"Okay, okay listen," Casey slurred a bit, the result of four drinks, and clapped her hands together. "I can't keep this in another minute."

Paige stopped mid-bite to listen. Michaela rolled her eyes. Koi kept shoveling the restaurant's famous crab cakes into her mouth like she'd never eaten out in her life.

"I have some news," Casey said mysteriously.

"Okay?" Michaela replied, tilting her head to the side.

Casey had everyone's attention. They all knew she was the Information Queen. When Casey had news, everyone had better listen.

Paige could see the slight tinge of nervousness creep into everyone's features. Would Casey's news be some sordid story about one of their famous husbands?

"We . . . meaning all of us BFFs here," Casey continued, darting her big, Betty Boop eyes around from face to face and hesitating like a game show host drawing heart-pounding suspense before the announcement of the grand prize.

Michaela kicked Paige under the table.

Paige gave her a crinkled-brow, motherly look that meant, "Be nice."

"We have been offered our own reality show!" Casey cheered, fanning her hands in front of her and bouncing in her seat. "Mina Lacks-Yousef, the mega-producer of all things reality T.V., wants us to join her Rich Wives franchise! We would be the Rich Wives of the Bronx."

Koi's fork hitting the plate was the only sound at the table. Paige quickly picked up the fruity drink Anwar had brought out earlier and threw it back so fast she didn't even taste it. There would be no more nursing that drink. Michaela's usually slanted eyes went round.

Casey looked around at their faces. "I know, right? Isn't this good news?" Casey asked with jolly confidence. "I mean, let's face it, this would be a golden opportunity for everyone here. I could use the exposure to broaden my platform, and I'm sure my boutique will be exploding with orders," she said, touching her chest proudly. She turned sideways to face Koi. "And you . . . Oh my goodness, you can finally get out from under Damien's shadow and have a camera crew following his sneaky butt at the same time. We know his reputation with the ladies."

Koi blinked, dumbfounded like she was thinking, *What reputation with the ladies?*

Casey faced Michaela now. "Michaela, we all know how you love to show off, right? And, with Rod retiring from football, you'll need something else to keep you relevant on the social scene. . . ."

Michaela opened her mouth to clap back, but Casey kept on speaking.

"And, Paige. Girl, you know you're my favorite. This would be just perfect for you. You need to come out of that little shell you live in. Get your own sense of self. I mean, with Antonio's basketball career being over and no trust fund from the great Senator Gladstone, you'll be able to keep things afloat this time."

A collective gasp flitted over the table. Suddenly, all eyes were on Paige.

Paige's color drained, and suddenly she was filled with a nauseating wave of disbelief. It was another punch from reality. She shot up from her chair and staggered slightly.

"Paige! Wait!" Casey called after her. She turned back to the women at the table. "What? What did I say? Didn't everyone already know?" Casey asked, her eyes big and genuine. "Does this mean she won't be on the show?"